Someone

The questions continued. The police roamed through her house, peering into corners. She didn't want them here. She wanted to be left alone.

Liam slipped his arm around her waist. "That's enough," he told the cops. "I'm taking her upstairs to bed."

Over their objections, he whisked her up the staircase and into her bedroom where he closed the door.

Crossing the room, she turned on the bedside lamp. Compared to downstairs, it was quiet here—creating the impression of a peaceful, safe haven. But it was only an illusion, a pipe dream. "I won't be able to sleep."

"Have you got a suitcase?"

"Of course."

"Throw some clothes in it. We're getting out of here."

ABOUT THE AUTHOR

Though Cassie Miles is now a city creature living in Denver, she once lived in a small log cabin in the Rockies with no television or running water. It was quite the starter home and the greatest place in the world to get away and read. She's still reading, of course. But it's hard to imagine those long-ago days of chopping wood, knee-deep snow and hauling water up the hill from the creek.

Books by Cassie Miles

CAST OF CHARACTERS

Kate Carradine—Hiding out in the mountains for twenty-eight days, she can't even remember her own name. Her only certainty is that somebody wants her dead.

Liam MacKenzie—He rescued Kate and will protect her. Though he loves her as a natural woman, the heiress side of her personality ticks him off.

Wayne Silverman—The family attorney disappeared in the mountains with Kate. Is he a victim, a criminal or both?

Elizabeth Carradine—Kate's mother is overwhelmed by the responsibilities of the family wealth and business.

Peter Rowe—Kate's stepfather enjoys a life of ease and comfort. What crimes would he commit to keep his lifestyle?

Tom Rowe—Kate's stepbrother is an expert marksman. As a glorified "gofer," he resents the Carradines and wants to get back at them.

Jonathan Proctor—Though divorced from Kate, he maintains his position as CEO of the family business. His life would be easier with Kate out of the way.

Mickey Wheaton—The ambitious reporter knows a lot about Kate and the family business. Perhaps, too much.

Adam Briggs—The head of Colorado Crime Consultants uses his resources to help Kate and Liam, but he's frustrated when they step outside the law.

Prologue

A raindrop splattered on her forehead. Another on her cheek. Her eyelids pried open, and she stared into a gray, stormy sky blanketed with clouds.

Lying flat on her back in a sloping field, her gaze lowered slowly. She saw distant peaks, a jagged cliff side and the edge of a dense, old-growth forest. She heard the rush of wind. *Where am I?*

Though she had never been here before, the terrain was familiar. Her fingers tightened on a clump of sweetgrass, and she smelled wild mint. The trees were mostly ponderosa pine, but there was also a stand of aspen with lean white trunks and the round green leaves of early summer. She knew that she was somewhere in the Rockies, probably in Colorado. *But why am I outdoors? How did I get here?*

Her brain floated—adrift in the hazy netherworld between sleep and wakefulness. Though she tried to think, she couldn't draw upon memory. The slate had been wiped clean.

And yet, she could identify the plants. Sweetgrass. Burdock. Snakeroot. Goldenrod. She recognized the charred stench that rose from her clothing; it smelled like an old campfire.

Instinct drove her to sit up. When she tried to stand, her body screamed in agony, and she sank back to the earth. Her legs ached from running, endless running.

Every muscle throbbed, but the pain was more intense on her left arm. She peeled off her parka to take a closer look. The upper sleeve of her blue silk blouse was shredded. Dried blood stained the fabric and there was a fresh red ooze. She'd been wounded.

Reaching up, she touched the back of her skull and found evidence of another injury. Blood matted her long, thick, blond hair. Something terrible had happened to her.

Her gaze swept the meadow. Amid the faraway line of conifers, she caught a glimpse of movement, and she focused intently. The barrel of a rifle aimed directly at her heart. They were coming for her! The hunters were coming.

A wave of terror surged in her chest, and she gasped. Her throat tightened. She was drowning in her own fear—an urgent panic that flooded every cell of her body. She had to escape. To run. To hide.

Rolling thunder echoed through the mountain cliffs and valleys, and the rain began to fall hard. Vertical sheets of water pelted her head and shoulders.

Drawing upon her last reserve of strength, she staggered to her feet. Beside her was a backpack—a big one that was suitable for weeklong wilderness expeditions. She hefted the weight onto her shoulders. She knew inherently that she needed to keep this pack with her at all times.

Stooped over, she moved as quickly as she could toward the nearby sheltering trees. Every step was torture. Inside her hiking boots, her toes cramped. Her knees and ankles creaked like frayed hinges.

At the edge of the forest, she collapsed on a carpet of pine needles. Small, gasping sobs escaped her chapped lips as she squinted through the rain toward the hunters on the opposite side of the mountain meadow.

She saw nothing. They were gone. She peered so intensely that her eyes ached. Nothing. They had vanished so quickly. Did they even exist? Had she invented the hunters? No! She knew they were out there.

Fear was her only reality, her only truth. People were after her. Faceless men, hunters, tracked her down like an animal. *My God, why? What have I done?*

If they found her, they would kill her. They'd tried once already. The slash on her arm. The wound on her head. She had to stay hidden, here in the forest. It was the only way she'd survive. She had to be smart. But how? How could she pretend to be clever when her brain was addled and her memory was gone?

She couldn't do this. It was better to surrender, to lie back and accept her fate.

"Stop it," she whispered angrily. She wasn't a quitter. Though she didn't remember her own name, she knew this: she wasn't the sort of woman who gave up without a fight.

Her shoulders straightened. She would take responsibility for her own safety. She would forge a new life, a new identity. Here, in the forest.

Following the custom of Native American tribes christening a newborn, she chose her name based on the first thing she had seen when she'd awakened.

Rain. I am Rain.

Chapter One

At midafternoon on a sunlit day, Rain hunkered down beside a rippling creek. She reached into the cold, clear water and picked out a pebble. Round and smooth, the stone was the color of a tiger's stripe and speckled with bits of quartz.

After careful inspection, she decided the tawny color was perfect for today—a very good day because she'd caught a fish. Today, she was fierce as a tiger. She was the huntress instead of the hunted.

Though she'd seen no sign of the men who had been pursuing her for days, she still felt their presence. At any given moment, they might appear.

Rain turned her back on the creek and scurried toward her wilderness home. Careful not to follow the same route and create a path that might lead others to her hideout, she zigzagged toward a wall of pines and a towering granite formation. Behind three fat boulders was a cleared space with a fire pit. She pushed aside a clump of sagebrush and entered her shallow cave.

Kneeling on the cave floor, she ceremoniously dropped the tiger pebble into a basket she'd woven from reeds and twigs. One pebble for every day of her new life. "Twenty-eight, so far."

Proud that she'd survived so long, Rain smiled. The sunburned skin across her cheeks stretched and cracked, and she rubbed her face. Without moisturizer, her complexion must be a leathery disaster. Not that she was planning to win any beauty pageants.

Her jeans were torn, and so baggy that she held them up with twine she'd plaited from reeds and sweetgrass. Her blue silk shirt was in tatters. Several days ago, she'd given up on grooming her long, unmanageable, blond hair and had hacked it short—not stylish but functional. She didn't have time to worry about how she looked. Every moment was dedicated to survival. Nothing else mattered.

Though it was a bit early for dinner preparations, she couldn't wait to cook the fresh trout that would go so well with her usual salad of goldenrod, burdock and mint. As she took the leaves from the cooking pot where they soaked in water from the creek, she wished that she had oil or butter for frying.

Those were food items her backpack had not provided, but she wasn't complaining. The pack had literally saved her life. Tucked inside, she'd found a Marmot Pinnacle sleeping bag, a serrated Buck knife, a collapsible fishing rod and Meals, Ready-to-Eat—the same kind of prepackaged, high-calorie food that the U.S. military used on maneuvers.

Though the last of her MREs had been devoured thirteen days ago, Rain found plenty of edible foods in the wild. Bark and grass. Flowers and roots. And now, the chokecherries and elderberries had begun to appear. She wouldn't starve.

In fact, her health was good. Her wounds had healed, thanks to the first aid kit in her pack and her knowledge of medicinal plants.

Though she still couldn't force herself to recall what had happened to her, memories had appeared like snapshots—moments caught in time. Once remembered, these pieces of the past became hers, not to be forgotten again.

Easily, she pictured her mother descending a sweeping staircase, being greeted by a golden retriever with a wildly wagging tail.

And there was a Little League game she'd coached.

On a green golf course, she practiced her swing.

Rain remembered her own wedding. The pristine lace dress. The filmy veil. And roses, tons of pink roses. Unfortunately, the groom wasn't a clear vision, and she had the sinking feeling that her marriage hadn't turned out well.

The elaborate, many-tiered cake, she recalled, had been delicious.

With a longing sigh, she fantasized about all the marvelous foods she used to eat. Gourmet sauces. Cheese and bread. Cream and chocolate desserts. She especially missed the candy bars her father used to bring home when she was a little girl. He'd hold out his arms and allow her to search his jacket pockets until she found the chocolate.

By far, her favorite memories were the days she'd spent with her father. A big, strong man, he'd taught her wilderness skills when she was a girl. They used to go backpacking together. He'd taught her how to forage; those skills had probably saved her life.

Through the mouth of her cave, she glanced heavenward. Her father—his name was Eric—had passed away several years ago. "I miss you, Dad."

In her mind, she repeated his name. *Eric*. The golden

retriever, also deceased, was Daisy. Her mother was Elizabeth. She'd remarried. Her new husband was Peter Rowe, and he had a son, Tom Rowe. All those names. But when it came to her own identity, she was still…Rain.

Knowledge of her immediate past remained elusive no matter how hard she tried to remember. The only thing she knew for sure was that hunters were trying to kill her, and their pursuit was relentless.

The only way to be safe was to stay hidden.

This was her life. The forest was her home. And it was time to build the fire and cook her fish. She took the cooking supplies from the backpack and went to the fire pit where the twigs and sticks were already laid.

Carefully, she guarded the flame of a match from her dwindling supply. For kindling, she used a hundred-dollar bill.

PILOTING SOLO IN HIS modified Super Cub, Liam MacKenzie swooped low and made a pass through an isolated valley in Rocky Mountain National Park. Not a particularly safe aerial maneuver, this dive wasn't anything he'd try with the people who regularly hired him as a charter pilot. But Liam had been flying this little Cub so long that she was like an extension of his own body; he could make her do anything he wanted. He tipped the wing and stared down at the waving grasses. There appeared to be nothing unusual.

Nearing the edge of the meadow, he pulled back on the yoke, cleared the treetops and ruddered left, preparing to make another sweep. Two days ago, he'd flown high over several miles of terrain, including this meadow, taking aerial photos for a real estate developer in Grand Lake. When he'd gotten the developed pictures back and studied them, he'd seen a parka on the ground—a sign of human life where none should be.

There were dozens of possible explanations. An animal might have dragged the parka there. Someone outside the sanctioned camping area might have lost their jacket. But Liam hoped the parka was a sign of two people who had been missing for nearly a month: Kate Carradine and her boyfriend, Wayne Silverman.

The major search-and-rescue efforts had ended a couple of weeks ago and miles away from here. A forest fire had destroyed nearly a thousand acres, and these two missing people were presumed lost in the flames. No trace of them had been found. No bones. No rubber-soled hiking boots. And, significantly, no sign of a burned-out vehicle.

The absence of a car gave rise to speculation that they hadn't gone camping in the first place, had never been in the area and didn't want to be found.

None of these theories satisfied Kate's mother, Elizabeth Carradine-Rowe, a wealthy socialite and—from what Liam had heard—a first-class pain in the rear. Miss Elizabeth couldn't believe that her only daughter had disappeared. She'd contacted Colorado Crime Consultants. Through CCC, Liam had gotten involved.

In a soaring loop, he brought his Cub around for another view of the mountain meadow. He volunteered his time and his plane for search efforts because he believed in CCC and in the founder, Adam Briggs. Their goal was pure: solving crime for the sake of justice and to bring closure for the victims' family and friends. Everyone who worked for CCC's loosely organized network was a private citizen with special expertise. There were doctors, medical examiners, coroners, meteorologists, entomologists and pilots like Liam.

He first became aware of CCC when he was an assistant district attorney in Denver. That felt like a lifetime ago! Seventy-hour workweeks. Three-piece suits. Courtroom battles. Constant stress. Yeah, there had been a few rewards. Like the satisfaction of taking a dangerous perp off the streets. But there had been a hell of a lot more frustrations.

On his thirtieth birthday, three years ago, Liam dumped his career and moved to Grand Lake to be a charter pilot. Wise decision.

Now his only association with crime was CCC. Purely voluntary. He operated on his own schedule, followed his own methods. Twice, his aerial photos had been instrumental in locating missing persons—both dead.

RAIN HUNCHED HER SHOULDERS and ducked down. The plane was coming back. She heard the whine of the propeller. He was making a second sweep. Though her fire was too small to be seen, and well-hidden by the surrounding forest, he might notice the rising smoke.

Her heart beat fast. He was one of them—one of the hunters.

She tasted bitter fear in the back of her mouth. If she tamped the fire or doused it with water, the smoke would billow. He'd know she was here.

Her gaze encompassed her cozy campsite. It felt like home, and she didn't want to leave. Damn it! If she was found, if the hunters came near, she would have to gather up everything and run.

But how could she escape unseen? There were hours of daylight left, and it would be easy for a pilot to spot her from the air as she made her way across the hillsides. There had to be another solution.

She went to her backpack and took out the gun.

As the Cub came around, Liam's gaze skimmed the distant peaks, still marked with snow in early August. He looked down on dense, old-growth forests and rugged cliffs. The noise of his plane's engine startled a small herd of elk, and they darted into the forest.

Liam dipped down across the open terrain again. There was a flash from the ground—something was down there.

This sighting merited closer investigation, but he knew better than to land in a meadow with high grasses that hid rocks and prairie dog holes. The low-pressure tundra tires on his Super Cub were made for rugged landings, but he needed to see the obstacles. He pulled up and looked for an open stretch—a couple hundred feet was enough.

Nothing out here resembled a landing strip. There were no roads, no houses, no ranger stations. This area was miles away from sanctioned campgrounds, seriously isolated.

Nearly a mile and a half away, he spied a dry, gravelly stretch beside a wide creek. A challenging descent, but he could do it. He aligned his approach and cut the speed, slowed until he was floating on air. Then the wheels hit the earth, and Liam jolted like ice in a blender.

The Cub lurched to a stop, and he leaned forward to fondly pat her dashboard. She was a good old girl.

Before leaving the cockpit, he stuffed a candy bar into the pocket of his plaid flannel shirt. Not much of a dinner, but it would have to do. He grabbed the photographs of the missing people and hiked due north.

Liam didn't expect to find them alive, especially not Kate. Her photo showed an attractive, pampered Colorado blonde with long, smooth hair and cool blue eyes.

She'd never last two days in the mountains, much less a month.

Pausing at the top of a ridge, he looked down at the mountain meadow. The sun hung low in the sky, and shadows had fallen across the land. He needed to hurry so he wouldn't have to take off in the dark.

Jogging down the slope, he tried to pinpoint the area where he'd seen a flash. After a lot of tromping around, he found it. A crushed beer can—the ubiquitous sign of humanity.

When he picked up the can, he realized that it hadn't been in this location for long; the grass beneath it was green and alive.

He followed a slight trail, marked by broken grasses. There was another can and three rocks piled on top of each other. What the hell was going on here?

Walking slowly, he came to a flattened area of grass. Someone had been lying here.

He squatted down to take a closer look. Caught in thorny shrub was a scrap of fabric. Blue silk. That was the kind of quality material Kate Carradine would wear.

When he stood, he caught a whiff of smoke. A campfire! What kind of moron would start a fire here? Too easily, the flames could spread. Danger of another killer forest fire was high. He hiked toward the faintly rising smoke, ready to kick some irresponsible camper's butt.

At the edge of the trees, he heard a shout.

"Don't come any closer! I have a gun!"

It was a woman's voice.

"Ma'am," Liam called out, "you can't have a fire here. It's dangerous."

There was no response. Did she really have a gun?

He called out to her again. "This isn't a sanctioned camping area."

"Are you a park ranger?"

He rested his hand against the trunk of a ponderosa pine and peered toward the sound of her voice. Though he couldn't see her, she appeared to be hiding behind three lichen-covered boulders. "I'm with CCC."

"Colorado Crime Consultants." Rain had heard of them. CCC was a volunteer group, and she knew intuitively that they were the good guys. If he was telling the truth, she could trust him. "What kind of work are you doing for CCC?"

"I'm looking for two missing persons."

"Who?"

"Their names are Wayne Silverman and Kate Carradine."

"Kate, huh?" The name resonated through her brain. She heard the faint echo of voices calling that name. Her name? "I suppose that's short for Katherine."

"Probably."

"Katherine Carradine. That's a long name," she said. Though familiar, she wasn't ready to accept that identity. "Six syllables. You'd think a person would remember a name that long."

"Ma'am? Is anybody here with you?"

Why did he want to know? Though she'd watched him approach alone, others might be with him.

The hairs on her nape prickled. Her head swiveled, trying to see in all directions at once.

Returning her attention to the tall man, her thumb twitched on the handle of the Glock automatic, and her trigger finger tightened as she kept her aim steady. Though she didn't want to shoot anybody, she might not have a

choice. He could be lying to her. He could be one of the hunters.

"What about you?" she shouted, keeping the tremor from her voice. "Is anybody here with you?"

"I'm alone."

"You came in a plane," she said. "I heard you buzz the field. You scared the wildlife."

He took a step toward the rocks where she was hiding. "Have you got a name?"

"You can call me Rain. One syllable."

"Nice to meet you, Rain. I'm Liam."

When he took another step, she growled, "Didn't you hear me? I have a gun, and I shoot trespassers. Now, back off. Walk away."

"It's not safe for you to have a fire out here."

As if he cared. If he was one of the hunters, he would burn her alive. Panic crashed inside her head. "I told you to stop moving."

"It's okay." He took another step toward her. "I'm not going to hurt you."

Like hell he wasn't. She aimed high and pulled the trigger. The gunshot exploded.

Chapter Two

Liam hit the dirt. This crazy woman was shooting at him! He sure as hell hadn't bargained for this.

"Hey, mister," she called out. "Liam? Are you all right?"

Cautiously, he raised his head and looked up. She stood on top of the boulders, only twenty feet away from him. A bizarre sight. She was skinny as a bone. Her jeans were torn at both knees, and she wore a baggy black T-shirt over a blouse with a blue collar. Blue silk? Her blond hair with dark roots stood out in wild spikes. Her face was darkly tanned, emphasizing her blue eyes. There was something about those eyes. A clarity. A steadiness that told him she wasn't really crazy after all.

She squatted on her rock perch, limber as a gymnast. "I couldn't have hit you. I aimed high."

"I'm okay." As he rose to his feet and brushed off his jeans, he continued to study her. Though she barely resembled the woman in the photograph, Liam knew he'd found Kate Carradine.

"It's you," he said. "You're Kate."

"I'm not. I already told you my name."

"Rain." It suited her. She was wild as a lightning storm

across the Rockies. He couldn't believe Kate Carradine had managed to survive in the wilderness. This was tough, rugged country, and she'd been here almost a month.

Finding her alive was some kind of miracle, and he was determined that he wouldn't leave without her. Though she looked wiry and strong, she might have been injured. Must have been. Why else would she stay here?

His first obvious step was to gain her trust so she'd allow him to come closer. If he could get her talking, he could convince her to leave. Feigning nonchalance, he said, "You're cooking something."

"I caught a fish." She sounded proud of herself. "That's my dinner."

"I'm hungry, too. Maybe we could share."

A frown creased her forehead. "I suppose I should offer my hospitality. That's the proper thing to do, to share whatever is mine."

"You're right," he said. "That's proper."

But when he took a step closer, she raised her gun again. Her attitude changed. "Normal rules don't apply out here." Her voice was firm. "I advise you not to come any closer."

Looking down the barrel of her handgun, he planted his feet and took root. "I'm not moving."

Her gaze darted as though searching for something. "I don't want to shoot you, but I will."

Approaching her was like trying to get close to a wounded mountain lion. She needed his help but refused to take it. She was scared. And, therefore, dangerous.

"I don't mean any harm." He needed to convince her that he was a friend. Reaching into the pocket of his flannel shirt, he took out the candy bar and held it up so she could see. "I'll make you a deal—put down the gun, and you can have this."

"Chocolate," she whispered. "Oh, how I've missed chocolate."

Her mouth watered. Her stomach growled. Never in her life had Rain wanted anything more than she wanted that candy bar. She wanted to inhale the sugary cocoa fragrance, to feel the gooey texture as it melted on her tongue.

This man—Liam—held the candy bar toward her. He was calm, unaware of the treasure in his hands. She swallowed hard, remembering her father and the candy bars he'd carried.

But she wasn't ready to entrust her hard-won safety to Liam. Though he said he was alone and worked for CCC, she didn't know for sure. He could be one of the hunters.

Still keeping watch on him, she glanced toward the meadow and the stream. The sound of her gunshot should have summoned other searchers, other hunters.

But she saw no one else.

Was it safe to take the chocolate?

No way would she allow Liam to come closer. He was a big man, over six feet tall. Though he was lean, his shoulders looked muscular inside his red-and-black plaid flannel shirt.

Her gaze zeroed in on the candy bar. "Do you have any credentials from CCC?"

"Nope. It's a volunteer organization."

"Then how do I know you're working with them?"

"You have to trust me," he said.

Not a chance. Not so easily. What if he was armed? She certainly couldn't get close enough to frisk him. Gesturing emphatically with her gun, she said, "Take off your shirt."

He set the candy bar down on the pine needles and did as she asked, peeling off the plaid flannel. A white T-shirt fit snugly across his chest. His upper arms were sinewy and strong. There wasn't an ounce of flab on his frame.

"Now," she said, "put your hands over your head and turn around in a circle. Real slow."

Though she should have been looking for a handgun or a holster fastened to his leather belt, she was distracted by his tapering torso and his tight, round bottom. She wanted to believe that he wasn't one of the men hunting her. But how could she be sure?

When he faced her again, she studied his features, looking for a reason to trust him. Or to know he was the enemy. He had a good, strong nose and firm jaw that made her think he was either stubborn or arrogant. What about his eyes? Eyes were the clearest indicator of temperament. His were deep-set, hazel in color. Though she was holding a lethal weapon, his eyes showed no fear. Instead, there was…determination? Curiosity?

"Empty your pockets," she ordered.

A muscle in his jaw twitched, and she could tell that he was irritated. But he did as she asked.

The contents of his pockets included a Swiss Army knife, but nothing else that could be considered dangerous.

Satisfied that he was unarmed, she said, "Okay, I'll take that chocolate now."

"It's my dinner," he said. "Do I get some of your fish?"

When she'd been a little girl, camping with her father, Rain had learned to share her bounty with anyone who showed up at the campfire. Wilderness hospitality meant looking out for each other.

Obviously, such protocol didn't apply to someone who meant to do you harm. Though Liam said he was on a search-and-rescue mission, she still wasn't convinced. She wouldn't give up her edge, no matter how attractive his butt. "Toss the candy bar over here, close to these rocks. Then, step back five paces."

Again, he followed her instructions.

As she climbed down from the boulders, her heart beat faster. The air grew thick with portent, and she felt a little bit dizzy. Interaction with another human being had jolted something loose inside her head. Another memory. Not a pleasant one.

A sense of danger flared, and the heat spread through her veins, melting her resolve, dragging her toward a dangerous weariness. She was losing control. *Fight it! Don't give in!* Bracing her back against the boulder, she faced the tall stranger.

"Are you all right?" he asked.

"I'm fine." Her voice quavered. "Stay back."

What next? It was hard to think. Her brain was in turmoil. She forced words through her lips. "Put your hands over your head."

He followed her instructions. The precious, beautiful, delicious chocolate was within her grasp, but she couldn't move. She stared at the center of Liam's chest. And she remembered....

A burst of gunfire. It crashed and rattled inside her head. She saw blood that wasn't her own. A man had been shot, fatally wounded. The thick, red blood spread across his chest as he staggered toward her.

Rain blinked rapidly, trying to clear this unwanted vision from her head. For an instant, she had seen the past with crystal clarity. And it terrified her.

She glanced down at the gun in her trembling hand, and she feared the worst. Had she fired the fatal bullet? Was she a murderer? In an awful yet logical way, it made sense. She hadn't hesitated to shoot at Liam. Had someone else threatened her?

Oh God, what if she was on the run because she'd killed another human being? What if the hunters who were after her were lawmen?

Rain needed to find out more, to unlock her memories. Right now, Liam was her only source of information.

"The names," she said. "Tell me again. What are the names of those missing people?"

"Kate Carradine," he said. "Wayne Silverman."

Had she killed Wayne Silverman? Though she couldn't visualize his face, there was no doubt in her mind that he had died. His spirit had departed from this earth. "What else do you know?"

"Wayne was your boyfriend." Liam's hands were still raised above his head. "Together, you left Denver and went to the mountains for a camping trip. There were several forest fires that weekend. When you didn't return on Monday morning, search parties started looking."

"A fire." When she had first come to this meadow, her clothing had smelled of smoke. It was becoming inescapably clear that she was, in fact, Kate Carradine.

"Let me help you," Liam offered. "I'll take you home where you'll be safe."

"Home?" But this forest was her home. If she returned to Denver, she would be walking into lethal peril. But how could that be? She'd be returning to her family. Her mother, Elizabeth. Her stepfather and stepbrother. Returning to their welcoming embrace gave her no comfort.

"Listen, Kate—"

"Don't call me that. I'm not who you think I am."

Liam raised his eyebrows. "You're Kate Carradine."

"No." She could take care of herself as long as she stayed here. This was her sanctuary. Loudly, she proclaimed, "My name is Rain. I live here. And I'm not leaving. Not ever."

In two measured steps, she approached the candy bar. Her intention was to retrieve her chocolate and take it back to her cave where she could eat it slowly and make the flavor last for days. But when she touched the smooth wrapper, her self-discipline faded.

One bite wouldn't hurt. Still holding her Glock, she tore open the wrapper with her teeth. The smell was heavenly. Her taste buds danced with giddy anticipation. She bit through the chocolate and caramel. A warm memory of her father's face flashed across her mind, easing her fear. Candy bars had only good, comforting associations for her.

Another taste. Chocolate smeared across her chapped lips. She licked it off and nibbled again.

When she looked up, she saw Liam watching her. He was grinning, and before she could stop herself, she returned his smile.

Just as quickly, she scowled. It was still too soon to trust him. "This isn't funny, you know. I've been out here for twenty-eight days."

"I'm not laughing." He knitted his fingers together and rested his hands on top of his head. "I like to see a woman who enjoys her food."

She took another small bite, savoring the texture. The sugar rushed through her system, boosting her energy, giving her a false sense of well-being. "All right, Liam.

What kind of work do you do when you're not flying search and rescue for CCC?"

"I'm a charter pilot based out of Grand Lake."

"Why did you come to this spot?"

"A couple of days ago, I took aerial photos of your meadow. When the pictures came back, I noticed a parka on the ground."

She nodded. He was telling the truth. Her parka had gotten wet and she'd laid it out in the grasses to dry. "So you came back to look around."

"That's right," he said. "Now, I have a question for you. Why do you want to stay here?"

"I want to be left alone."

"Something's got you scared," he said.

His perceptiveness surprised her. Her eyes narrowed as she met his gaze. "Why do you think I'm afraid?"

Steadily and calmly, he said, "You're hiding from something. Why?"

This was more than enough sharing of information. Even if Liam wasn't one of the hunters, she wanted him gone. Rain had no intention of leaving these mountains.

She'd nibbled the candy bar down to a stub, which she held out toward him. "The rest is yours."

As he approached, she realized her mistake in inviting him closer. Before she could pull the candy bar back, Liam took it from her. And he kept on coming.

She scrambled backward until she was trapped between the boulder and this tall, muscular man. He must be nuts to come at her like this. Didn't he see the Glock? The barrel was only inches away from his belly. If she pulled the trigger—

He grasped her wrist and bent her elbow. The bore of the gun pointed toward the sky. His body pressed against hers. She could feel his hard strength and the heat that emanated from him. This was her first human contact in weeks, and the sensation startled her. She'd forgotten what it was like to be touched.

His nearness took her breath away. His fingers locked firmly around her forearm, and his gaze imprisoned hers.

"I could disarm you." He wasn't bragging, merely stating a fact.

Her lips pressed tightly together. There was no point in objecting. Liam was capable of physically overpowering her.

"However…" His voice was deep and resonant and—God help her!—sexy. "I'm not interested in taking your gun away."

Up close, his hazel eyes were flecked with gold and deep, forest green. He stared with an unblinking intensity that verified her earlier impression: this was a stubborn man. She asked, "What do you want from me?"

"The truth," he said. "You could have returned to civilization if you wanted. You seem to be healthy enough to hike out. But you stayed here, and I want to know why."

Rain swallowed hard. "I don't have a simple explanation."

"We've got time to talk," he said. "Without having you wave a gun in my face."

"Fair enough."

When he stepped back and released her, the gun lowered to her side. The fact that he had released her, rather than press his advantage, counted for a great deal. Though still wary, she had to believe that he meant her no harm.

"Come with me." Rain circled around the boulders and led him into her little camp. He was the first person to see her wilderness home.

"Very nice," he said.

She was proud of what she'd done here. The gravelled area in front of her cave was neatly groomed. This was her dining room and kitchen. She'd cleared away the foliage and built her fire pit against the rocks. Using stones and a sturdy pine branch with the bark whittled away, she'd made a spit across the fire. Though she hadn't managed to catch any fresh meat to cook on her spit, she used the branch to hang her only cooking pot above the flames. The water in the pot churned at a slow, erratic boil.

She offered, "Would you like some tea?"

"Sure."

Luckily, she had two cups—one of which she used for brushing her teeth by the creek. She poured water into the toothbrush cup to rinse it out.

"What's that?" he asked. "The thing you're using to hold your water?"

"It's a sock."

"I can see that. Why isn't the water draining through it?"

"Because it's lined with a condom."

"Ah." A sick expression pulled down the corners of his mouth. "And where did you find condoms?"

"In my backpack." She pointed to three other condom-socks hanging from tree branches. "Handy little things. They hold about a quart of water each. Does that seem excessive to you?"

"Not if they're elephant condoms."

She dipped boiling water from the pot into each cup and added her own special mixture of sage, sorrel bark and mint. "We let it steep. Then, it's tea."

He asked, "Is this all the food you've had to eat?"

"I had seven MREs. Those lasted for about two weeks."

"Meals, Ready-to-Eat. Like in the Army." Liam leaned against a boulder beside the fire. "So you packed for a week's worth of camping."

"I had all the basics."

Whether or not she'd packed these items herself was an unanswered question. Surreptitiously, she glanced toward the expedition-sized backpack that leaned against the inner wall of her cave. In addition to the camping gear, the bottom of the backpack had been lined with neatly wrapped bundles of hundred-dollar bills. Almost fifty thousand in cash. There had also been a pouch containing jewelry—diamonds and gold.

Rain had tried and tried to come up with reasonable explanations for why she might be carrying money and gems on a camping trip. Unfortunately, she kept coming back to the same conclusion: this loot was stolen. Which made her a thief. If she added that fact to the revelation that she was also possibly a murderer…

"What else was in your pack?" he asked.

No way would she tell him about the treasure. "A hunting knife. Fishing kit. Sleeping bag. That cooking pot. And first aid supplies, thank goodness."

"Were you injured?"

She rolled up the tattered sleeve of her silk blouse and the T-shirt she wore on top of it. A wide, red scar crossed the middle of her upper arm. "This was bad at first, but I used antiseptic from the first aid kit. And I made a poultice from valerian leaves and roots to draw out the infection. I'm not sure if that was the right herb, but it seemed to help."

"Was that your only wound?"

She reached up and rubbed her hand through her spiky hair. "I had a bump on my head. No big deal."

Liam knew that head injuries could be tricky. If she'd had a concussion, it might explain her strange behavior. "You should see a doctor."

"I'm already healed," she said blithely. "No infections."

"Kate, you have to go back," he said gently. "Sooner or later, you need to let your family know you're all right. Your mother's worried."

"When you leave, you can tell her that I'm okay."

"She wants you to come home. She's the one who convinced CCC to continue the search."

An expression of concern crossed her face, and her gaze turned inward, as though she were reviewing her options. Then, she shook her head. "No," she said simply. "This is my home. I'm safe here."

"Safe from what?" he asked. "Why do you think you're in danger?"

"I just know."

She handed him a cup of fragrant mint tea and returned to the fire. She wasn't insane. Her little hideout was orderly and efficient. Her ability to survive required an intelligent application of concentration and knowledge.

But she had completely disowned her prior existence; she refused to be Kate Carradine. "Is somebody after you? Who is it?"

She whipped around to face him. Her fists planted on her hips. Her voice was a challenge. "I can't remember."

That didn't make a whole lot of sense. If she'd been scared enough to stay in hiding for nearly a month, she must know why. "Are you saying that you can't remember their names?"

She met his gaze. "I can't remember anything. When

I first came here, my memory was completely gone. The slate was wiped clean."

Son of a bitch! She had amnesia.

Chapter Three

As Liam studied the defiant woman who stood before him, he realized that handling Kate Carradine would require a delicate touch. He couldn't fling her over his shoulder and haul her out of the forest. He needed to overcome her resistance and convince her to cooperate. Not an easy proposition.

When he'd worked for the Denver district attorney, he'd honed his skills in interrogation, and he was pretty damn good at knowing when someone was telling the truth. But how could he deal with amnesia? He wasn't a psychologist. "You don't remember anything?"

"Nothing about the immediate past." She squared her thin shoulders and gave a diffident shrug. "It's not really important."

"The hell it isn't."

"If I can't remember, what difference does it make?"

"Let's start with the obvious fact that Wayne Silverman is still missing. Your memory might be able to explain what happened to him."

"I can't tell you." Her gaze flickered, but she didn't look away. "I'm sorry that my disappearance triggered a search-and-rescue effort. And I'm sorry that I caused people to worry. But I didn't have a choice. I'm in danger."

"From a person or persons unknown."

"That's right," she said.

. He sensed that her amnesia masked darker, more sinister events. Something traumatic had happened to her—something too terrible to remember.

If he hoped to uncover the truth, he needed to keep her talking. "Fill me in on what you do remember. You came here twenty-eight days ago. Wounded."

"I wasn't exactly here," she said. "It took me a while to find this perfect little cave."

"But you don't remember where you came from."

"I was on the run."

"But you didn't plan to go into hiding," he said. "You only had enough food for a week."

"That's when the MREs ran out," she said.

"So you lived off the land," he said. "How did you know which plants were edible?"

"It's not difficult. There are obvious ones to stay away from. Vetch. Locoweed. And the state flower, the columbine." As she talked, she returned to her food-preparation tasks, lifting a cover of leaves from an expertly filleted trout and placing the fish in the boiling water to poach. "There are ways to see if a plant is poisonous."

"Like what?"

"Cut off a little piece and put it between your teeth and your gums. If it starts to sting or cause some other reaction, spit it out."

Her story intrigued him. He was familiar with mountain-survival techniques but had never known anybody who actually lived off the land. "How did you learn all this?"

"My dad," she said. "He used to take me backpacking and we'd forage for dinner."

"Makes sense. Your father was the head of RMS, Rocky Mountain Suppliers." He hadn't taken that piece of her background into account. "He specialized in outdoor equipment."

"I remember." The minute she mentioned her father, her attitude brightened. "When we went camping, we were always testing some kind of gear. Dad used to say he was the luckiest man in the world because camping was a business trip for him. He loved the mountains."

"Eric Carradine," Liam said. "And you're his daughter, Kate."

"Rain," she said. "Call me Rain."

"Okay. It's Rain." He decided to humor her. So what if she wanted to call herself Rain? Or Moon? Or Ruby-Throated Hummingbird? After all these days in the wild and a dose of amnesia, some delusional thinking was to be expected.

Besides, her Rain persona appealed to him. He respected and appreciated her gutsy stamina. In her identity as Kate Carradine, he expected her to be a socialite, a pampered society woman who arranged flower bouquets rather than eating them for dinner.

"There's plenty of food out here," she said. "Look at all these trees. Inside the new branches is a soft, woody part that's edible. If you roast pinecones in the fire, then break them open, these little nuts fall out."

"Sounds like a lot of effort."

"Oh, it is," she said. "I spend most of the daylight hours foraging. And I have to hike all over the place to do it because I don't want to completely wipe out the ecosystem in front of my cave."

"Because it's bad for the environment?"

"And I didn't want anybody to find me." She poked at the fish in her cooking pot. "Why don't you sit down and relax?"

Though he had the feeling that he was losing focus on his goal of getting her away from this place, Liam allowed himself to be seduced. He sat on a flat rock at the opposite side of the fire pit and watched as she efficiently arranged leaves and stems on a woven plate made from twigs.

"You made those plates," he said.

"When I figured out how easy it was to weave young branches and reeds, I made a bunch of things. It gave me something to do at night, when I couldn't forage."

Given enough time out here, he suspected she might really create a home for herself. Her little space was swept clean, and she'd placed dried flowers among the rocks for decoration. He pointed to a tall woven vase just inside her cave. "What's that?"

"My calendar." She brought the woven vessel closer so he could see inside. "There's one pebble for every day I've been here. I try to choose a rock that looks like the day."

He reached inside and ran his fingers through the stones. "I see several black ones."

"Dark days." Hunkered down opposite him, she plucked out a caramel-colored stone. "This is today. It reminded me of a tiger, and that seemed appropriate because today I caught a fish. I was a huntress."

"And you held me at bay," he said.

"Yeah." She gave a self-deprecating wink. "I'm really fearsome, huh?"

"I wouldn't use that word to describe you."

"No? What word would you use?"

"Resourceful," he said. "Smart."

She cocked her head to one side and grinned. "Keep going."

When she wasn't holding a gun on him, she had a vivid charm and enthusiasm. "Pretty."

She rolled her eyes. "Now you're making fun of me."

"I'm not," he said. "You look good to me."

"Apparently," she drawled, "you don't get out much."

But he wasn't lying. He thought she had a great, expressive smile. And he liked the healthy tan color of her skin that contrasted with her cornflower-blue eyes. Even the weird hairdo worked for him. With the dark roots, and blond on top, she reminded him of some kind of exotic, tufted bird.

She passed him a plate with a miniscule shred of trout and weedy leaves. He took a taste. The flavor of the roughage was a cross between grazing and gnawing on a tree limb, but it'd be ungrateful not to eat the food she'd gone to such trouble to gather and prepare.

Rain attacked her plate with gusto. Though she wasn't transported into ecstasy, like when she'd eaten the candy, she took regular bites and chewed thoroughly.

She glanced at his plate and raised an eyebrow. "Not hungry?"

"I eat slow."

"If you don't finish your greens, no dessert. That's what my mother always used to say."

The mention of Elizabeth Carradine-Rowe reminded Liam of his mission. He needed to get Kate out of here.

Glancing through the sheltering trees, he saw that dusk had begun to settle. Soon it would be too dark for him to attempt a takeoff in the Cub. "I can't leave after dark," he said. "I can't see the hazards to the plane."

"Tonight will be dark," she agreed. "It's a new moon tonight, only a skinny crescent."

"Come with me. We can go now while there's still enough light."

"How many times do I have to say no?"

"I won't leave without you."

"Then we have a standoff," she said. "You can't force me to come with you. And, it seems that I can't make you go."

He set his plate aside and leaned back against the boulder, settling in. "Guess I'll have to spend the night."

For an instant, her eyes sparkled. He could tell that she was enjoying his company, no matter how resistant she pretended to be. "Don't think—for one minute—that you'll be sharing my sleeping bag."

She stacked his plate on top of her own and went about her business, briskly informing him about the rules of the camp. No more wood on the fire. Food scraps must be carried far away and buried so they wouldn't attract animals during the night. "And if you need to, um, relieve yourself, go a long way from camp. I don't want the smell around here."

"We don't have to do this," he said.

"I'm sure there are other ways, but I prefer—"

"Come back to Denver with me," he said. "Tonight you could sleep in a bed. With a soft comforter. You could take a long, hot shower."

"Not interested."

The light was fading. He had only a few minutes to convince her. "What about your memory? A psychiatrist could get it back. Hypnosis or something."

"It might be better if I don't remember." Her words held a disturbing ring of truth. "All I need to know, deep in my heart, is that I'm in danger. I'm the prey, and there are hunters coming after me. Can you trust me about this?"

"I trust you, Rain."

Her face lit up. "You called me Rain."

"The name suits you."

He was drawn toward her by a compelling force. More than anything, he wanted to make her smile again and again. He wanted to hold her, to protect her from danger—be it real or imagined.

As she sat near him, the faint glow of sunset and the dying campfire illuminated the planes of her face. Her full lips parted as she breathed, softly and steadily. Gentle shadows outlined her high cheekbones and her sharp jawline.

Rain. He was struck by the realization that he liked this feral woman. He admired her gritty determination, no matter how misguided.

"Just for the sake of argument," she said, "tell me what you know about Kate's family."

"The Carradines are a legend in Denver. Old money."

She gave him her full attention. "So we're rich."

"Very."

Liam tried to remember all that he could. In the early 1900s, the Carradines started with a general store. Kate's grandfather turned it into a successful franchise of outdoor-sporting-goods outlets, Rocky Mountain Suppliers.

"And my father?"

"He took the business worldwide."

From RMS, the Carradines built an empire with varied dealings in land development and housing, both in Denver and the mountain resorts. Though they sponsored charity events, RMS wasn't known for their efforts to protect the environment.

"That can't be right," she said. "My dad was concerned about the environment. And so am I. In fact, I was working on a project. It was a wilderness camp for disadvantaged kids. My primary contact person was Rachel Robertson, a fantastic woman who runs a homeless shelter."

"Like I said, RMS is involved in charities."

"What else?"

Unfortunately, Liam had run out of things to tell her. He reached into his shirt pocket and pulled out the photographs. "This is you. And Wayne."

She stared for a full minute at the photo of herself, then she sighed. "You're right. I am pretty. At least in this picture."

Then she looked at Wayne Silverman. "He's an attorney, but I don't think he was ever my boyfriend. Maybe we dated."

"When you disappeared, you were planning to spend the weekend with him."

"Camping." She looked up at him. "That doesn't mean we were sleeping together."

"Do you have any idea where he is?"

Her expression turned guarded. "Not a clue."

Liam knew she was keeping something from him, and her secret was connected to Wayne Silverman.

She crossed the small clearing and grabbed the strap of her backpack, which she pulled deeper inside her cave, where he couldn't see. Was she trying to keep the pack away from him?

She emerged carrying a silver solar blanket which she held toward him. "You're sleeping on the ground tonight. But you can use this to ward off the chill."

"I'm not tired."

"Me neither. But after it's dark, we need to sleep, to keep strong for another day of foraging."

That was what she thought. But if Liam had his way, tomorrow would be the day when she finally went home.

RAIN AWOKE AT DAWN AND opened her eyes only a slit, just as she had last night when Liam had crept into her cave. She'd seen him sneaking toward her and noticed how his eyes focused on the backpack that rested at her feet. His intentions seemed clear: he'd planned to rifle through the backpack.

Searching for information? Or had he known about the jewels and cash? As she had lain inside the sleeping bag, her muscles had tensed.

Then he'd turned around and left her cave.

She'd spent a couple of sleepless hours trying to figure out why he hadn't grabbed her backpack. Even if she'd tried to stop him, they'd already established that he was physically superior and capable of taking control. Why had he backed off?

The reason, she'd finally decided, was simple: Liam was a decent person who respected her privacy. Even though he was incredibly curious, even though he wanted her to return to Denver, he wouldn't force his opinion upon her.

Her eyelids opened wider. The soft, pinkish glow of dawn flowed into her cave, and a hint of dewy moisture hung in the air. Such a fine way to start the day! She would miss these mornings.

Nonetheless, Rain knew it was time to leave her mountain habitat; she couldn't deny that she was Kate Carradine from an old-money family in Denver. While Liam had talked and shown her the photographs, memories of her former life had taken root in her consciousness. She had to go home, to face whatever awaited her in the city.

After sleeping on it, her decision was made. It was time.

Rolling to her stomach, she gazed across the cleared area to where Liam should have been sleeping under the silver solar blanket. She didn't see him.

Where was he? Throwing aside the sleeping bag, she emerged from her cave and went to the three boulders that sheltered her campsite. After a quick scan of the meadow, she spotted Liam's red plaid shirt down by the stream. Even at this distance, she noticed the breadth of his shoulders. A mountain man. He was comfortable here…almost as much as she was.

Rain decided to use this time alone in camp to handle an important task. Returning to her cave, she knelt before the backpack and unzipped the bottom pouch. Stacks of hundred-dollar bills tumbled onto the earthen floor. Though she'd already used some of this paper money for kindling, the cash made a good-sized package when she wrapped it tightly in a T-shirt. At the deepest part of her cave, she crammed the bundle into a crevice, then added the pouch full of diamonds and gold. For extra security, she rolled a heavy rock in front of the hiding place, then smoothed the dirt with her hands.

This stash was her insurance policy. If she'd stolen it herself, the treasure was safely tucked away from the police. If, on the other hand, the hunters wanted to get their hands on the cash and jewelry, she had a bargaining chip. Only she would know where it was hidden.

As she came out of the cave dusting off her hands, Liam returned. He looked at her dirty fingers. "Making mud pies for breakfast?"

"Just tidying up," she said. "After thinking about

everything you told me last night, I've made my decision. It's time for me to pack up and leave."

He rewarded her with a huge smile, and she thought for a moment that he was going to hug her. "You made the right decision, Rain."

With a sigh, she said, "I guess you should start calling me Kate."

"All right, Kate. By coming back, you're going to make a lot of people happy."

"Not everybody." For the hunters, her return would not be cause for celebration. "If you don't mind, I think I should ease back into civilization gradually."

"Not a problem," he said. "We'll go to my cabin first. It's fairly remote. You can take a shower, have some solid food and get your bearings."

"I can't wait."

BY THE TIME LIAM BROUGHT his Super Cub around for a landing on an unmanned airstrip in the mountains, Kate was bubbling with excitement, unable to decide which delightful thing to do first.

"I want bacon and eggs for breakfast," she said. "And a candy bar for dessert."

"We can do that."

She beamed. All the food in the world was available to her. The idea of going to a grocery store and picking out whatever she wanted seemed utterly astonishing.

"And a shower," she said. "And clean clothes."

"You got it."

Liam would also make sure her family was notified that she was safe and well. He wondered why she hadn't immediately thought of them but chalked her indifference up to amnesia.

The Cub touched down lightly and slowed. Liam maneuvered until he had the small plane backed up in front of a rough, wooden shed with a door wide enough for the wingspan. He cut the engines. "I'm not going to put her in the hangar. I've got my Land Rover parked in back. I was doing a little work on her."

She peered through the windshield. "Is this your property?"

"The cabin's back there in the trees."

When her feet touched the packed gravel, she felt weightless, as though they were still in the air. Kate hitched up her baggy jeans and followed him toward a neat little two-story log cabin with a sloped shake-shingle roof and a wide porch across the front.

"Very nice," she said, echoing his comment when he'd seen her cave.

"Like I said, it's remote."

The terrain was rugged, little more than a clearing in a dense conifer forest. A craggy cliff side formed a natural boundary at the western edge of the grassy field.

She noticed a battered old Jeep with a snowplow attached to the front. "I thought your car was in the hangar."

"The Rover is parked indoors. I only use this Jeep to clear the road and the airstrip. I'm on the edge of national forest, and the regular plows don't come up here."

"The end of the road," she said. "You like your solitude."

"Love it." On the porch, he pulled his keys from his jeans pocket and unlocked the front door. "What do you want to do first? Food or shower?"

"Shower," she said emphatically. "I haven't felt hot water in twenty-eight days."

He whisked her through a living room with a stone

fireplace and heavy furniture. "The bathroom is back here. Take your time."

"I don't suppose you have any clothes that might fit me."

"As a matter of fact, my twelve-year-old nephew was up here for a week. I think he left some stuff." He opened the door to a linen closet and rummaged through the lowest shelf. "Here we go. Jeans and a T-shirt."

One glance at the tiny jeans convinced her that they'd never fit. And the T-shirt was emblazoned with voluptuous blue lips and gothic-style print. "Does that say Death Wormer?"

"I think it's Darth Vermin," Liam said. "They're not his favorite band anymore. Which is why the shirt was left behind."

Though she doubted the little-boy clothes would fit, she accepted them with thanks and entered the bathroom. Hesitantly, Kate sidled toward the mirror above the sink. She wasn't going to be a pretty sight. For twenty-eight days she'd been without moisturizer, body wash, shampoo or conditioner. Her only cleansing products were toothpaste—thank goodness she'd had that—and a large bar of soap which she'd used sparingly, to make it last.

Avoiding the inevitable moment when she confronted her reflection, she turned on the water faucet. Hot water was a luxury she would never take for granted again. She held her hands beneath the flow and slowly washed away the dirt. Her palms felt rough and calloused.

Slowly, she lifted her chin and faced her reflection. Her matted, multicolored hair looked like porcupine quills. Her skin was dirty brown and her eyes seemed huge and wild. She was skinny, seriously scrawny. There was no meat on her cheeks, and the line of her jaw was razor sharp. Her neck was a twig.

She peeled off her clothing. Her hip bones jutted out. Her breasts were almost nonexistent.

Apparently, living off the land was a terrific weight-loss program. However, if the end result meant looking like this, Kate doubted anyone would rush to sign up for a wilderness health spa.

"It could be worse," she told her reflection. "You could have turned green and grown scales."

But she didn't hate the way she looked. In her eyes, she saw a brand new confidence that she'd never had before. Her twenty-eight days in the mountains had given her time for growth. She was wiser—strengthened by the knowledge that she could take care of herself and survive against overwhelming odds.

Life would be different now. She was Kate Carradine, a pampered heiress who had regular appointments for facials, manicures and stylists.

She reached toward her reflection. Her fingers touched the mirror. "Goodbye, Rain."

Chapter Four

While Kate showered, Liam threw together a sandwich. His mood was pensive and concerned. He'd dragged Kate halfway back to civilization. Now he had to figure out what came next.

The problem was Wayne Silverman. He was still missing, and Kate was, most likely, the last person who had seen him. She was a witness. As such, Liam should have turned her over to the authorities for questioning.

But she was also a victim who was scared to death. She needed protection. His protection.

Her need was enough reason for him to bend the rules and keep her safely hidden away at his cabin. She wouldn't be much use as a witness, anyway. Not while she couldn't remember what had happened.

Her memory loss was the second big problem. Amnesia wasn't much of an alibi; the police would be skeptical. And when the media got hold of her story, all hell would break loose. Might as well call the tabloids right now.

Things would go a lot easier for Kate if she could remember. Last night, when he'd talked about her family, she seemed to have recall, and it stood to reason that more data might jog her memory. Photos and articles. The kind of information that Colorado Crime Consultants might have on file.

On the kitchen phone, he punched in the number for CCC. The office manager, Molly Griffith, greeted him warmly. Though they'd only met once, she remembered him. "You're the pilot from Grand Lake. What's up?"

"Is Adam there?"

"He's out on a case. I can help."

To tell the truth, Liam was relieved to be talking to Molly instead of her boss. Briggs was a stickler for following the letter of the law. No way would he approve of Kate staying at Liam's cabin.

"I found Kate Carradine," he said.

"Dead or alive?" Molly was blunt and straightforward. He suspected that she was all too accustomed to hearing the worst about missing persons.

"Very much alive," he assured her. "Kate's in good physical condition."

"Un-freaking-believable!" Molly enthused. "She's been missing for nearly a month. It's amazing that she survived. Where are you?"

"My cabin."

"How long will it take you to get here? I'll call her mother right away and—"

"Hold up," Liam said. "I want you to wait before making the notifications. Kate's scared and confused. She can't remember what happened to her."

"Amnesia?"

"Exactly," he said. "I need a day or two to calm her down."

"You know we don't work like that," Molly said. "CCC always cooperates with the cops."

"It's not the police that worry me," he said. "There's going to be a media frenzy. Kate needs time to prepare herself."

There was a pause on the other end of the phone while Molly considered. Then she said, "One more day can't hurt."

"Thanks, Molly."

"Adam won't be happy about this plan, but I'll convince him." Molly had a lot of brass. She needed a strong personality to deal with her boss. "What can I do to help?"

"Like I said, she has amnesia. It'd be useful if Kate could see more information on the Carradine family. Fax me anything you have. Photographs would be good."

"I put together a file when her mother contacted us," Molly said. "Consider it faxed."

He disconnected the call, finished off his sandwich and made himself another. After only one night on Kate's regimen of weeds and bitter tea, he was starving.

Sandwich in hand, he went outside and stood on the front porch to eat. The view always gave him pleasure. He owned eight acres, but the surrounding national forest made his location seem vast. His nearest neighbors were 2.7 miles down the road, and they weren't often home. Still, he was able to drive into Grand Lake in about half an hour, and he had all the comforts. His solitude was nothing compared to Kate's experience.

With the second sandwich devoured, he went back into the house and headed toward his office to pick up the faxes from Molly. As he passed the closed bathroom door, he didn't hear noise from the shower. "Kate? How are you doing in there?"

"You wouldn't happen to have a blow-dryer?"

"No."

"Mousse?"

"Sorry."

She opened the door. "I'm sure mascara is out of the question."

She looked damn cute in his nephew's jeans and T-shirt. Though she was skinny, her curves were unmistakably feminine. Her waist was tiny, and her butt filled out the denim quite nicely. Though her hair was still spiky from being wet, her overall appearance was more tamed. "You look good."

"Not hardly," she said. "I don't care what the Duchess of Windsor said about how you can't be too thin or too rich. This is too much."

"Too much thin? Or too much rich?"

"I don't know about the rich part. You seem to think my family is loaded."

He remembered his initial destination: the fax machine in his office. "We'll find out."

She leaned toward him. Her nose crinkled as she inhaled. "You smell like a ham sandwich. I want one."

Stepping inside his office, he scooped a handful of pages from the fax. He wasn't surprised by the speedy response; Molly was efficient.

Then, he led the way to the kitchen. "There's the fridge. Help yourself."

She stood with the refrigerator door wide open. "Everything. I want everything."

Moving at warp speed, she grabbed bread, mayo and lunch meat. Before she put together a sandwich, she was distracted by an orange which she juggled from hand to hand before biting into the rind. In seconds, she had it peeled. Two sections popped into her mouth. The cheese

didn't reach the countertop. Kate folded the slice and devoured it.

"Potato chips!" She snatched the bag from the counter
and ripped it open. A couple of chips followed the cheese.

Liam stepped back to avoid being accidentally con-
sumed by this human eating machine. He sat at the
kitchen table and watched with amusement as Kate sam-
pled bites of everything she touched. Like a kid given free
rein in a candy store, she was tempted by each item, and
she ate with blissful abandon.

But it only took a few minutes before she stopped.
She placed her hand on her flat stomach and said, "I'm
already full."

Her eyes were so mournful that he chuckled.

"All this great food," she said, "and I can't fit more
than a couple of bites inside me."

"There's plenty of time," he said. "Take a break. You
can eat more later."

"True." She brought a can of soda to the kitchen table,
popped the tab and took a sip. "I love fizzy things. Soda.
Seltzer. Champagne."

"You're a little fizzy yourself," he said.

Her smile of pure satisfaction gratified him. He'd
never seen a woman so pleased by so little. He wished
they could have more time together. Just the two of them.

As she licked the salt off a potato chip, she circled the
table to stand before him. "I'm glad you convinced me
to leave the mountains."

When she leaned toward him and patted his cheek, he
inhaled the clean fragrance of soap and shampoo. The
electric blue of her eyes sent a jolt through his body. He
wanted to pull her closer, to taste her mouth, to discover
if she kissed with the same appetite she showed for food.

"Thank you, Liam." Her voice was soft and a little breathless. "You rescued me."

"You were doing okay on your own."

"But you came along at exactly the right moment." Her smile was honest, warm and fresh as…Rain.

When she had been Rain, she'd belonged solely to him. He was the man who had discovered her, the only person who had seen her mountain cave. He wanted to keep her for himself. In Rain, he had met a woman who matched, even surpassed, his need for quiet and solitude. A woman who embraced the mountain life. A wild woman who was tough, gutsy and not afraid to be alone.

For now, Liam needed to deal with her other identity.

"All right, Kate." He handed her the faxes. "I contacted CCC, and they sent some photos to help you remember."

She sat at the table and looked at the photograph on top. "A wedding picture."

Kate recognized herself in that gorgeous, lacy gown. Then she looked at the face of the groom. "Jonathan Proctor," she murmured. "We're divorced."

"Sorry," Liam said.

"Don't be. It wasn't a good marriage. We did a lot of fighting."

Unpleasant memories flowed like a river across the parched surface of her mind. She and Jonathan had seldom seen eye to eye. He'd coped by shutting down and refusing to speak, except to criticize.

She had a very clear image of herself and Jonathan sitting at opposite ends of a long, ornate table. Neither of them said a word.

"The divorce," she said, "was practically the only thing we agreed about. He still works at RMS. In fact, he's the CEO."

Liam gave her a disbelieving look. "Are you telling me that your ex-husband runs the Carradine family business?"

"He's good at his job, and I hardly ever see him. Jonathan handles the business and development projects. My work is on the charitable side."

As she focused on a photograph of herself and a Little League baseball team, a pleasant warmth rose inside her. She enjoyed working on fund-raising events, many of which were athletic in nature since Rocky Mountain Suppliers was, essentially, a sporting-goods company.

Pointing to a group photo, she picked out a face. "This is Rachel Robertson."

"You mentioned her before," Liam said.

"She runs a homeless shelter, and she's helping me with plans to set up a mountain camp for disadvantaged kids. Some of the money from the RMS summer gala was going to finance it."

"The summer gala?"

"It should be happening in a couple of weeks." If the plans for the gala had been derailed by her absence, Kate would never forgive herself. Several charities depended on contributions raised by the formal dinner, dance and silent auction. "It's a black-tie event."

"Not my style," he said.

"Maybe it should be. You'd look great in a tux."

Actually, he'd look great in almost anything. As Liam gazed down at the faxed pages, she studied his profile. Dark stubble outlined his firm jaw. Beneath his rugged brow, his deep-set, hazel eyes glowed with health.

He pointed to a picture. "Are these the Williams sisters, from tennis?"

"Venus and Serena," she said. "Right."

"And you're standing between them. You were in good shape."

The photo showed her as a sunshine blonde in a white tennis dress. Her teeth were perfect. Her skin was perfect. She wondered if she'd ever be so carefree again.

With Liam, she sorted through other photos of celebrity golf tournaments and tennis matches. For nearly an hour, she stared at picture after picture, waiting for a memory revelation that simply wouldn't come. "It's no use," she said. "I can't remember why I needed to stay in hiding."

"Maybe more food."

"Always a good solution."

They took a break and made hamburgers. Liam took his turn in the shower.

Then, it was back to the photos. Kate picked up another wedding photo. It was her mother with her husband of two years, Peter Rowe.

Liam said, "It might help you remember if you talk your way through these pictures."

She nodded. "This is my mother, Elizabeth. She remarried two years ago. His name is Peter."

"And?"

"He's a handsome guy, kind of reminds me of Robert Wagner. He seems to make my mother happy, but I never really liked him. Probably, I resent him because nobody could ever take the place of my father. Especially not Peter."

"Why not?"

"Dad was totally into the outdoors. Peter is all about designer shoes and monogrammed shirts. He's happiest with a crystal champagne flute in his hand. He used to call me The Brat."

"You don't seem bratty to me," Liam said.

"I have a temper," she admitted. "A legendary bad temper."

"Like when you took a shot at me?"

"I wasn't angry then," she informed him. "Shooting trespassers is practical."

His grin was ironic but also charming. And she was comfortable enough to respond with a smile of her own. Comfortable. Peaceful.

She glided a fingertip across the smooth maple of the tabletop. She liked being here. His cabin was cozy and quiet. She'd forgotten how pleasant it was to be inside a warm house, sitting on a padded chair, drinking soda pop. Nice and normal.

She exhaled a sigh. "Before you came along, I had convinced myself that I'd never leave the forest. Now, here I am. In a cabin. With you."

He reached across the table. His large hand rested atop hers. "I'm glad you're here."

Though she suspected that Liam was only being kind and reassuring, she couldn't help wondering if a deeper relationship was possible. She wouldn't mind if he pulled her close in an embrace. It wouldn't hurt her feelings if he kissed her.

Oh, good grief! Was she falling for the man who had rescued her? Wasn't that the biggest cliché in the world?

"I still can't believe it," she said. "Yesterday, the most important thing was to catch a fish."

"Tomorrow will be harder," he said. "You'll have to face the media."

"And my family."

"You don't sound happy about that." His eyes were curious. "Does meeting your family worry you?"

"I feel terribly guilty. They're going to be angry and…" Her voice faded as a prickle of fear teased the edge of her consciousness. Why would she be scared of her own family?

"Back to the memories," she said, picking up a picture of herself with her stepbrother. "This is Tom. Peter's son. He's gotten interested in the family business, attends board meetings and usually is on my side."

"Does the board have a lot of disagreements?"

"Of course we do. RMS has a lot of money."

"Tell me about Tom. Is he athletic like you?"

"There's only one sport he excels at. Tom is an expert marksman."

Staring at the slightly blurred fax, she remembered a site trip with Tom. They had been looking at several mountain acres proposed for development. Her stepbrother had insisted on bringing his rifle, a Remington. In her mind, she saw him bracing the stock against his shoulder. Peering intently through his shaggy, dark brown bangs, he'd aimed and…

Gunfire rattled through the forest behind her. The shooters came nearer and nearer, but she couldn't see them. An oppressive weight pressed down upon her. Her arms were heavy. She couldn't carry on. Not one more step. Her legs ached. She sank to the earth, beaten. Sweat poured down her forehead. She couldn't move but she had to go forward. Into the flames. Into the searing fire.

"Kate, what is it? What do you remember?"

"A forest fire." Her memory faded. "It seemed like I was in the middle of it."

"Go on," Liam encouraged.

"I was carrying something."

"Your backpack?" he suggested.

"Heavier." She shook her head. "I can't see it. This is more like a feeling."

"What else?"

"The hunters," she said. "I don't know why they're after me. Damn it, why? What did I do wrong?"

"You didn't do anything," Liam said.

But her backpack held stacks of hundred-dollar bills and a pouch of jewelry. She remembered a man being shot. In her mind, she saw his blood. "What if I did? What if I'm a criminal?"

"I'd be surprised," he said. "You don't fit the typical profile for a perp."

"A perp? How do you know about perps?"

"Remember, Kate, before I moved to Grand Lake, I worked for the Denver D.A.'s office."

He'd been a prosecutor—not the best person to tell about possible criminal activities. Nervously, she asked, "What's the perp profile?"

"Not you," he said. "You're from an upper-class background, haven't been in trouble with the law before and you're socially active."

She took a potato chip from the bag on the table and studied it before nibbling at the edge. "None of those things are a guarantee that I wouldn't do something I might regret."

"Everybody is capable of lapses in judgment." He tipped back in his chair. His arms folded across his chest. Those sexy hazel eyes steadily regarded her. "You've brought up the topic of criminal behavior a couple of times. Why?"

Because I might be a thief. Or a murderer. She looked away; it wasn't easy to withhold information from him. "I can't tell you."

"Can't? Or won't?"

"Both," she said. "Do you think I'm crazy?"

"I can't answer that question until you tell me the whole truth."

She wasn't ready. Not yet. Not until she was certain that she hadn't shot Wayne Silverman or stolen the loot that was now buried in her cave. "I'm not lying to you."

"But you're holding back."

His scrutiny made her nervous. She got up from the table, walked a few paces, then turned toward the front windows. "I need to go outside. I'm feeling cooped up."

"Holding back information will do that to you."

Liam shoved back his chair and rose from the table. Her refusal to come clean was beginning to tick him off. What was she hiding? He wanted to help her, to believe her. But he didn't have the patience to play evasive games.

On the front porch, he leaned against the railing and looked out on his land. Lazy clouds drifted across the afternoon skies. At the end of the day, the pace of life slowed to a crawl. Even in the mountains, where there were no time clocks, the squirrels took a recess from their constant foraging and the birds returned to their nests.

Liam glanced toward his Super Cub, gleaming white in the sunlight. Probably, he ought to move it inside the shed. But it didn't look like rain. The Cub would be okay for the night.

Besides, they'd be taking off early tomorrow, heading back to Denver. Kate had to return to her family. He'd probably never see her again. In the life she'd been describing, there was no place for a man like him.

"It's odd," she said. "We've only known each other for twenty-four hours, but it feels like a lot longer."

"A lifetime." Long enough for him to be annoyed with her.

Her sharp chin lifted as she stared straight ahead, concentrating on an unknown future beyond the horizon. Her short hair ruffled in the breeze, and the corner of her mouth pulled into an adorable little frown.

His irritation faded. He'd known her long enough to forgive, to accept her shifts in attitude. Long enough to know that he liked this woman.

"Can I ask you a favor, Liam?"

He nodded.

"When we get to Denver," she said, "promise me that you won't leave me alone."

"You don't need me to hold your hand."

"I'd feel safer if you stayed with me."

He couldn't deny her request. If she truly was in danger—a possibility that he was beginning to doubt—he would protect her. Grudgingly, he promised, "I'll stay at your side. For a while."

But not for long. His place was here, in the mountains. Once they got to town, she'd slide back into her upperclass life. Kate Carradine would be fine. Just fine.

Suddenly, her back stiffened. Her thin neck craned. "Someone's coming."

He glanced toward the road. "I don't think so."

"Listen. They're getting closer."

"Kate, you're mistaken."

She grasped his arm and tugged at his sleeve. "Can't you hear the birds? We need to get out of here. We've got to run."

Chapter Five

When he looked into her wide blue eyes, Liam saw fear that bordered on panic. Unreasonable fear. Terror.

Kate wasn't playing games anymore. She had sensed the approach of danger. After twenty-eight days in the wilderness, her instincts were honed.

But this time, Liam thought, she had to be wrong. He tried to explain. "Even if there is a car on the road, they aren't coming after you."

"We haven't got time to talk."

Rationally, he continued, "Kate, I only made one phone call to CCC. Nobody else knows you're here."

She grabbed his hand, dragging him down the stairs and off the porch. "We've got to hide."

Though he could have argued, it was simpler to let her have her way. If, in fact, someone was driving up the road to his house, he and Kate could watch from the hillside. When the visitors arrived, he'd show her it was safe. Then, they'd come back to the cabin. No harm done.

"This way." He took the lead, hiking up a pathway that wound through the boulders to an overlook. Most people would have been winded by the swift, steep ascent, but Liam knew the land. And Kate was agile as a mountain goat.

They reached a ledge where they were hidden in the trees. "Better?" he asked.

"Higher." She peered up the hillside. "We should go higher."

Liam heard the sound of a vehicle on the graded gravel road leading to his house. Damned if she hadn't been right! "No time. Lie flat on your stomach across this rock. We can see the house and the field from here. Nobody will see us."

She stretched out beside him. Side by side, they watched as a pickup truck pulled up in front of his house. Two men sat in the back. Both carried rifles.

Another two emerged from the cab and strode toward the house.

"Anybody home?" one of them yelled.

The others laughed raucously, as if he'd said something clever.

Liam didn't recognize these men, but they looked like they could have come from a local tavern in Grand Lake or Eldora. All wore jeans and boots. All were armed.

They sure as hell weren't trying to be subtle. They swaggered. They yelled like schoolyard bullies who were all talk and no action.

The tallest guy, a redhead, turned to the others. "I'll do the talking."

"Aw, man! If you get revved up, we'll be here all damn day."

The redhead snarled back, "Are you saying I got a big mouth?"

"I'm saying you ain't the boss."

Their voices carried on the thin air. Though Liam and Kate were over fifty yards away, they could hear every word.

The sound of stomping came from Liam's porch. "Kate Carradine!" he yelled. "We know you're in there!"

The redhead lowered his rifle, sighted down the barrel and blasted a hole in Liam's front window. The glass shattered.

"Bastards," Liam muttered.

He glanced toward Kate. Her thin shoulders trembled. These were the hunters, the men she feared. Seeing them had to be her worst nightmare come true.

Painfully, Liam realized there was no way he could stop them. He hadn't taken her seriously, hadn't bothered to arm himself.

The only way they'd be safe was to stay hidden. But how? Those rifles had scopes. If these guys had half a brain, they'd scan the hillsides.

When all four disappeared into his cabin, Liam tapped her shoulder and whispered, "You were right. We need to go higher."

Kate didn't need further encouragement. She was on her feet, following him into the trees. Liam moved at a quick pace, dodging between the tree trunks as he traversed the slope, putting distance between them and the house. This rugged hillside was his backyard, and he knew the quickest routes, the best vantage points. When they emerged from forested land, he guided her higher. Loose gravel crumbled beneath their hiking boots. Too much noise! They were making too much noise.

"Up here." Clinging to the edge of jagged, lichen-covered boulders, they climbed. Though they couldn't see the house from here, they were directly above the shed he used as a hangar for his Cub.

Nestled against the boulder, he held her close and whispered into her ear. "Do you recognize them?"

"Hunters." Her breath came in ragged gasps. "They're coming for me."

"Have you seen them before? These specific men?"

"I don't know."

The blast of a rifle shot echoed through the forest like a shock wave. What the hell were they shooting at? Another window? The cabin walls?

A whimper escaped her lips, and she covered her mouth with both hands.

Until now, he'd only seen her terror in momentary flashes. He'd heard it in the way she spoke of the hunters. But her fears hadn't seemed real to him. There was no longer reason for doubt. Kate's mysterious hunters had set upon them, loudly and violently.

He encircled her slender body with his arms. Silently, he vowed to protect her with his last ounce of strength.

From the direction of the house, one voice sounded more loudly than the others. "Where the hell are you, Kate Carradine?"

"They must've took off for Denver," one of them remarked.

"Damn straight," another one said. "They ain't here."

Through the trees, Liam saw a flash of red hair as two men approached the shed he used as a hangar. He turned slightly, shielding Kate with his body.

"I'm telling you," one voice said, "they ain't here."

"Damn it all. If we don't bring her back, we don't get paid. They're here. Hiding someplace."

"I ain't climbing all over looking for them."

The redhead let loose with a string of profanity. "Hey! You think if I shoot this airplane it'll explode?"

"Always does in the movies."

"Let's do it."

Liam's muscles tensed. As the rifles popped and bullets pinged, rage exploded behind his eyes. These braying jackasses were shooting up his Cub.

If Kate hadn't been with him, Liam would have charged down the hill and torn these mindless, vicious idiots limb from limb. Not the Cub!

"I'm sorry," she whispered.

"Shh."

The worst thing that could happen now was if the gun-toting morons found them. But Liam didn't think that would happen. These guys didn't have enough brain-power to organize a search. The real villain was whoever had sent them—the person who promised a payoff if they brought Kate to him.

The foursome tromped around in circles, yelling back and forth, unable to figure out any sort of strategy. Idiots! Bastards! Mindless, ass-brained, flea-infested good old boys!

Though adrenaline surged through his body, Liam didn't make the mistake of thinking he could take them. Their very stupidity made them lethal.

Finally, they got bored, gave up and left. Their pickup bounced along the graded road, leaving a cloud of dust and needless devastation.

A slow-burning anger took root in Liam's heart. This vandalism would not go unpunished.

Kate tugged on his shirt, and he looked down into her eyes. The fear was still there. "They'll be back," she said.

"We're not going to wait around for them."

He stood, pulling her upright with him. Still tense, the heat of his fury surged through his veins. He was on fire inside. When he held her against his chest, she was ice-cold, shivering as though her blood had frozen.

Stroking her fragile shoulders, he whispered, "You were right, Kate. Somebody's trying to kill you."

"I wish I'd been wrong. I wish none of this had ever happened."

Her voice quavered, but she wasn't crying. He could feel her battling for self-control, willing herself to be strong. She'd been through hell. Hiding out for nearly a month, she'd lived with danger every single day.

"Nobody's going to hurt you," he promised. "I won't let them."

No matter what, he'd protect this small, brave woman. He lightly kissed the top of her head. She was delicate as a wounded baby bird. Her desperate need fueled his resolve. Nobody would hurt her. Never again.

At the foot of the hillside, he caught sight of his Cub. One white wing glistened in the sunlight. Liam's anger sharpened to a knifepoint. Somebody would pay for this senseless destruction. He had a damn good reason to track down the bad guys.

Though Liam had been hard-pressed to find anything positive about the assault on his cabin, he supposed they'd been lucky that the rifle-toting thugs had spared his Land Rover. They'd shot out the windshield on the Jeep parked at the front of the cabin. But they hadn't bothered the Rover, which had been in the back of the hangar. He'd loaded up Kate and taken off fast.

After two hours' drive, they were approaching Golden, a couple of miles outside Denver. Though the city of Golden had spread into upscale suburbs and develop-ments, the center of town kept an old-west facade which was in direct contrast to the sprawling Coors Brewery, a huge tourist attraction offering free beer. Golden was also the gateway to Lookout Mountain, where Buffalo Bill Cody was buried.

Liam glanced over at Kate in the passenger seat. She'd been silent for most of the drive, turned in upon herself. And he'd been glad when she'd dropped off for a nap. The road ahead of her promised to be rocky and difficult—not to mention dangerous.

Now she was awake, and she gasped at the first panoramic view of Denver. City lights spread across the plains in twinkling splendor beneath a vast, dusky sky of gray.

"I'm coming home," she said. "I should be glad."

"But you're not?"

"All I can think of is how much I'd rather be in the mountains."

Liam didn't bother with glib reassurances. "You're not going to be safe until we find out who's after you."

"What if I never remember?"

"There are other ways to figure this out."

His determination was twofold: find out who was threatening her, and protect her in the meantime. The handgun she'd used to threaten him—a Glock automatic—was in the glove compartment of his Rover, and Liam wouldn't hesitate to shoot. His Cub had sustained serious damage, and the interior of his cabin was trashed. Insurance would handle the repairs, but that wasn't the point. He wanted revenge.

"Why are we going to CCC?" she asked. "They were the only people you talked to. Obviously, they're in on this."

"I don't believe that." Adam Briggs was a good man, dedicated to finding the truth. He would also be Liam's first choice for someone to stand beside him in a fight. "I think their phones are bugged."

"Who would do that?"

He hated to point out the obvious. "Your mother was the person who contacted CCC and asked them to keep searching."

"My mother?" She shook her head. "Mom and I aren't cuddly and close. We've had more than our fair share of arguments. But I don't think she wants me dead."

"Other people in your family, or close associates, would have known that she'd contacted CCC. One of them might have bugged the phones."

"What if you're wrong? What if the hunters came from CCC?"

From what he knew of CCC, they weren't often involved in active investigations. They'd have no reason to suspect a bug. "Nobody at CCC wants to kill you."

"And someone in my family does?" She drew a ragged breath. "It's hard to believe that."

There were three men she'd mentioned: Her ex-husband, Jonathan Proctor. Her stepfather, Peter Rowe. And her stepbrother, Tom Rowe. In Liam's mind, those were the three main suspects.

He parked on a side street outside a two-story Victorian house with neatly tended flower beds in the front yard. This quaint, refurbished building was the unlikely office for CCC. Though it was after eight o'clock, lights shone through the windows.

He used his cell phone, punching in the office number for CCC. Molly answered.

"It's Liam," he said.

"I'm so glad you called. I've been trying to reach you at the cabin."

"Where are you?" Liam asked.

"Still at the office. Adam's here, too. Needless to say, he's annoyed about the Kate Carradine situation. He thinks—"

Liam disconnected the call. After reaching into the glove compartment and arming himself, he nodded to Kate. "We're going inside."

In the glow from a streetlight, he saw her face clearly. With a conscious effort, she erased the vestiges of fear. Her gaze became sharp and focused. "I can do this."

Her determination reminded him of Rain, and he smiled. "You're not alone anymore. I know you're telling the truth, and I'm with you, every step of the way."

They entered the building and went directly through the first door on the left into the offices of Colorado Crime Consultants.

Molly Griffith stood behind the front desk. She was a tall, sleek blonde in her midthirties, and she dressed a lot sexier than a typical office manager.

Walking firmly in spike heels, she rounded her desk. "You must be Kate Carradine."

"I must be."

"Good to finally see you." Molly enveloped her in a hug. "I can't tell you how many times I looked at your photograph and prayed you'd be okay."

Adam Briggs stepped through the door of his private office. Tall and muscular, with military bearing, he was nowhere near as warm as Molly. "Liam, what the hell did you think you were doing? This woman needs to be—"

"Don't start," Liam warned. "A couple of hours ago, my cabin was under assault from men who were looking for Kate Carradine. They trashed my cabin, and shot up my Super Cub. And the only place I had called was here."

Briggs lowered his eyebrows in a scowl. "Nobody else saw you or heard from you?"

"Nobody. We flew to my cabin without stopping anywhere else." Liam pointed to the phone on Molly's desk. "One call."

"A bug," Briggs growled. "You think somebody tapped my phone line."

"The whole damn office could be bugged."

While Molly fussed over Kate, her boss tore apart the handset on the desk. He found a small, silver disc. "Son of a bitch. This isn't even high tech."

"Not on this end," Molly said as she took it from him. "But this device could be programmed to pass information to a computer. Any search could be screened to show references to Kate Carradine."

"Like checking e-mail," Liam said. That was how the bastard had known she was at his cabin. And he'd acted quickly, sending his thugs.

Molly said, "We need to sweep the office for bugs."

"We'll make a full report to the police," Briggs said.

"And to the sheriff in Grand Lake," Liam said.

"No." Kate stepped forward. "There's nothing the police can do. We were never close enough to get a license plate from the truck that showed up at Liam's place. And I still don't remember enough to—"

"You'll make a report," Briggs said. His tone brooked no argument. "May I remind you, Miss Carradine, that Wayne Silverman is still missing. He is possibly the victim of foul play."

Her lips pressed into a thin line. Finally, she gave a curt nod. "You're right. I owe it to Wayne Silverman to make a full confession to the authorities."

Confession? Liam frowned. What was she talking about?

Chapter Six

As Liam drove, Kate peered into the darkness at the edge of the well-lit highway. Out there—beyond this tunnel of light—crouched the shadowed foothills, rife with nocturnal hunters and prey. Though she couldn't see the barn owl as it dived through the night and snatched a scurrying rodent, Kate could feel the wind from widespread wings. The hunters were coming closer every minute, and there was nothing she could do to stop them.

If Liam was right about her family being responsible for sending the men who shot up his cabin and his airplane, she was walking blindly into the arms of those who wanted her dead.

They were on their way to her mother's house.

Kate wanted to be angry—outraged—by the threat to her safety. Instead, a dull sadness filled her heart. What kind of life was she living? What could possibly turn a family member into a killer?

"The police have leads to follow," Liam said. "If Molly's theory about the bug broadcasting to a computer is correct, the cops can get a warrant to check all computers."

"At my mother's house?"

"That's right."

"Don't count on it," she said. "My family has a lot of clout. One of the charities RMS supports is the Police Benevolent Fund. My mother plays bridge with the governor's wife. It's going to take more than a suspicion to get a warrant on the Carradines."

"Politics." Liam's jaw clenched. "I remember this crap from when I worked for the D.A.'s office."

The stonewalling had already started. Adam Briggs had insisted that Kate talk to the police before anyone else. But he'd been overruled. The detectives in charge of the case had readily deferred to her mother. Kate was going home. The police would meet her there.

Approaching the exit ramp, she braced herself, unsure of what to expect and fearful of what she might remember. After another few turns, they were on the two-lane road leading to the house where her family had lived for the past eighteen years. Her memory of this place was crystal clear. Even in the dark, she recognized the landscape of home. It seemed as though she'd never forgotten these streets or the rising glow of porch lights on the ridge or the hedges and the landscaped stands of conifers.

"Turn right here," she instructed. They circled a long, paved driveway to a sprawling, two-story Tudor-style home with a dark brown shake-shingle roof. Every light was lit, and the multipaned windows sparkled in the night.

Liam parked near the entryway. "You're home," he said.

She should have felt relief. Home ought to mean safety. Instead, she was nervous, tense, scared. She grasped Liam's arm. "Stay with me. You're the only person I feel safe with."

He rested his hand upon hers. His eyes were warm and reassuring. "I won't abandon you. Not ever."

"I want to get away from here tonight. To go home to my own house. To sleep in my own bed."

"We can make that happen."

"It won't be easy," she warned. "My family can be very domineering."

Liam gave her a cool, determined smile. "So can I."

The front door opened, and an attractive blond woman emerged. Kate's mother, Elizabeth, would never do anything as unsophisticated as running, but she approached quickly. The gray silk scarf she wore around her throat streamed behind her in the evening breeze.

Kate stepped from the car and into her mother's perfumed embrace. A sigh fluttered from her mother's lips. Elizabeth Carradine was a complex woman. She could be ethereal, completely out of touch with reality. Other times, she was solid as a bulldozer, demanding that things be done her way.

"I never gave up hope," Elizabeth whispered. "I couldn't bear to lose you, darling. Not you, too."

"I'm okay."

Elizabeth held her at arm's length and studied her. A fey smile lifted the corners of her mouth. "What have you done to your hair?"

"I couldn't take care of—"

"Darling, do you really have amnesia?" Elizabeth leaned close to squint. Her eyes reminded Kate of when she'd been a little girl, sick in bed, and her mother would wish away the illness with a lullaby and a cup of honeyed tea. It was always the nanny who'd called the doctor. "Kate, darling. You remember me, don't you?"

"Yes, Mom."

Elizabeth lifted her chin and tossed her scarf over her shoulder. "What's all this nonsense about losing your memory?"

"It's nothing," Kate lied. She didn't want to cause her mother any more worry. "Just a little glitch. I can't remember exactly what happened before I set up camp in the forest."

"Well, that doesn't sound healthy." Elizabeth scowled, and a bevy of tiny wrinkles creased her forehead. "You need some tea. Chamomile, I think."

Liam stepped up beside them. "That's a fine idea, ma'am."

Elizabeth gave him a quick assessment, scanning his denim shirt and broad shoulders. "You're the young man who found my daughter."

"Liam MacKenzie." Kate introduced him.

Apparently, her mother had decided that Liam was acceptable. She grasped Liam's large hand in both of hers. "Thank you for rescuing my Kate."

"She didn't need much rescuing," he said. "Kate was surviving very well on her own."

His words sparked a warm feeling of pride within her. Kate wasn't a victim, and she sure as hell wasn't going to start acting like one. She had to take control, and Liam would help her. He'd back her up. "Come on, Mom. Let's go inside."

Before they could walk the few paces to the front door, chaos descended. Briggs and Molly parked behind Liam's Rover on the circular drive. Two police cars arrived with red and blue lights flashing.

Kate's stepbrother, Tom, drove up behind the cops, leaped from his car and loped toward her. His shaggy brown hair fell so low on his forehead that his eyes were hidden. He came to a stop in front of Kate, peering through his bangs. He seemed to want to embrace her but held himself back.

And she didn't open her arms to him. Her recent memory of Tom aiming his Remington rifle was too vivid in her mind. Those guys who had attacked Liam's cabin were just the sort of morons Tom would hang out with.

He regarded her with something akin to suspicion. "You're okay?"

"Yes," she said. Was he disappointed? "I used the wilderness-survival techniques my father taught me."

"Living off roots and berries?"

"It's not berry season, Tom. Except for huckleberries, and there weren't any—"

"I get it." He reached out and clumsily patted her arm. "Damn, Katie. I thought you were dead."

His words echoed hollowly inside her. Had Tom expected her to be dead? Could her own stepbrother have hunted her?

Though Tom had only been in the family for two years and was still something of an outsider, he generally supported Kate in family discussions and in business. More than once in the RMS boardroom, Tom had voted with her.

She pulled away from him, unsure of what she could or couldn't believe. Everyone was talking at once, and the noise disconcerted her.

She felt a hand on her shoulder and turned to face her stepfather, Peter Rowe. A total contrast to his son, Peter was tanned and perfectly groomed. In his butter-yellow polo shirt and khaki trousers, he looked like he'd just finished eighteen holes under par.

A familiar surge of hostility went through her, and she

quickly suppressed it. She shouldn't blame Peter for marrying her mother. By every indication, he made Elizabeth happy.

"It's good to have you back with us," he said.

"Good to be back." Her response was automatic.

Tom grasped her arm and pulled her toward the house. "You need food, Katie. Your mom probably doesn't keep any chocolate in the house, but I'm sure the cook can find something."

"Wait." She planted her feet, refusing to be drawn deeper into this swirling eddy. She needed her anchor. Only Liam could keep her from drowning in a well-intentioned undertow.

He stood slightly apart—tall and strong and amazingly calm. She thrust her hand toward him, reaching for a lifeline. And he came forward, linking his large hand with hers. As long as he was with her, Kate would feel safe.

NEARLY AN HOUR LATER, Liam sat beside Kate on a plaid sofa in an opulent room she referred to as the "den." A gleaming oak desk stood sentinel in front of a floor-to-ceiling display of hardbound volumes so perfectly aligned that they might have been painted on the wall. Two plainclothes police detectives sat like bookends in captain's chairs at either end of the sofa.

Kate spoke first. "We're wasting our time, detectives. I can't remember how I got to the place where I set up camp."

The husky, blond detective who identified himself as Clauson from Homicide nodded calmly. "Just a few questions, Kate. Let's start with your plans for the weekend you left on your camping trip. What's the last thing you recall?"

She fidgeted impatiently, reminding Liam of a wild animal trapped inside a cage. Her hands were in constant nervous motion, plucking at her clothes and combing through her short hair. She'd refused to change from the boys' jeans and the Darth Vermin T-shirt.

Though she'd managed to drink a few sips of a blended protein shake, she'd also avoided food. Kate seemed to be keeping her distance from everyone but him.

"Wayne Silverman," she said. "I was going somewhere with Wayne."

"The man who disappeared," Clauson said.

The man who was likely dead. Nobody had yet said that Wayne Silverman was deceased, but Detective Clauson was from the homicide division.

Kate reached over and caught Liam's hand. Ever since they got to her mother's house, she'd been constantly touching him, as if to reassure herself that he was still here. Her repeated physical contact was beginning to have a totally different effect on him.

She looked into his eyes. "What should I say?"

"Tell the detectives about your relationship with Silverman."

"We dated, but he wasn't my boyfriend." Her gaze turned inward. "Wayne regularly attended RMS board meetings. He worked for the outside legal firm that oversaw quarterly audits and tax problems."

When Kate focused, she was an intelligent woman with coherent business opinions. It was important, Liam thought, for her to show this face to the police so they wouldn't dismiss her as a crackpot who hid out in the mountains for no good reason.

Though he knew that the threat to her was as real as

the bullet holes in the fuselage of his plane, his opinion didn't matter. It was important for the cops to take her seriously.

She'd fallen back into silence, and Liam encouraged her. "You and Wayne were friends."

"I liked him. He supported me and my stepbrother, Tom, on environmental-protection issues. That's been a major topic in our recent boardroom discussions. Over the years, RMS has acquired a lot of mountain property. Jonathan wants to develop those lands."

"Jonathan?" Detective Clauson questioned.

"My ex-husband. Jonathan Proctor. He's the CEO."

"A powerful man," Clauson said. "You, your stepbrother and Wayne Silverman have been voting him down."

"Wayne didn't have a vote," she said. "His reasons for not supporting development were based on finance and legal issues. Tom and I were acting on environmental concerns. Like my dad, we both feel that enriching RMS isn't sufficient reason to tear down trees and put in roads. Not even when the EPA has given the go-ahead."

"That must have made Jonathan angry."

"Angry enough to kill me?" She scoffed. "Very doubtful. There were times, I'm sure, when Jonathan wouldn't have minded seeing me dead, but not since the divorce. We've gotten along fairly well for the past year."

"Maybe he was jealous of Wayne Silverman," Detective Clauson said.

She shifted uncomfortably on the sofa. "What are you suggesting?"

"You've said that someone was after you. That's why you hid out in the mountains."

"Correct," she said.

"There was an attack at Liam's cabin," Clauson continued. "And Adam Briggs confirmed that the phone at CCC was bugged."

"Correct again."

"Ma'am, I'm trying to find out who's responsible."

"I don't know."

"Your ex-husband—"

"Look here, Detective. Until I remember exactly what happened, I'm not going to accuse anybody. Jonathan— and the other members of the RMS board—are civilized men in three-piece suits. Our disagreements are friendly. Understand? Friendly. Before I left for the camping trip, Jonathan and I played on the same foursome in golf."

"Who won?" Liam asked, hoping to lighten her mood and keep her talking.

"I did. By two strokes." A grin spread across her face. "I kicked Jonathan's butt."

"Did he take it like a man?"

"Absolutely. He stomped around, threw his clubs and chugged a beer. Just like a man."

Clauson chuckled. His manner was easygoing, but Liam knew there was a sharp mind behind that bland expression. Before this session with Kate, Liam had given Clauson a brief, preliminary statement on what had happened when he'd located Kate, and the subsequent vandalism at his cabin.

Skillfully, Clauson directed Kate back to the original topic. "For your camping trip with Wayne Silverman, what did you pack?"

"I don't exactly remember." She shrugged. "My backpack got lost somewhere along the way."

Clauson glanced toward Liam. "I thought you had camping supplies with you."

"From Wayne's pack," she said. "At least, I think it was Wayne's pack."

"Do you remember driving into the mountains?"

"No."

Her grip tightened on Liam's hand, and her spine stiffened. He could almost see the memories coming back to her.

"What do you remember, Kate?"

"It was Wayne's car. Black. I think it was a Ford Explorer. I remember driving on a back road. My arm hurt really bad. I held the steering wheel tight."

Her hands rose in front of her as if she were gripping the wheel. Her eyes squinted as she struggled to see into the recent past. "There was a fire. Orange flames. Pine trees turned black. They cracked. Snapped like matchsticks. So much smoke. I could smell the smoke. I coughed and…" Her voice trailed off.

Liam and Clauson and the other detective leaned forward, concentrating on her words and gestures, willing her to remember.

Kate shook herself and sank back on the sofa, exhaling a heavy sigh. Her tension faded. In its wake, she seemed exhausted. "I woke up in a meadow, and it was raining."

"Are you sure," Clauson asked, "about the car?"

Her head bobbed up and down. "I was driving Wayne's Explorer."

"Driving in the mountains? You're sure?"

"Absolutely."

Liam asked, "What's the problem, Detective?"

Clauson spread his hands apologetically. "Wayne Silverman's car is parked in the garage at his town house."

Liam asked, "Any evidence that the vehicle had been near a fire?"

"The car's clean. I mean, spotless."

Kate rubbed at her eyes. "I don't understand."

Unfortunately, Liam did understand. He'd been with the D.A.'s office long enough to understand the weight given to tangible, physical evidence. Wayne Silverman's car was parked in a garage and clean. If Kate had been driving near a forest fire, the police would expect to find damage, ranging from scratches on the exterior to the lingering smell of smoke. Furthermore, she'd said her arm had hurt. If she'd been wounded, there ought to be blood on the upholstery. Therefore, her memories were unreliable. Her credibility with the police had been damaged.

Liam stood. "That's enough for tonight, detectives. Kate needs her rest."

Neither Clauson nor his silent partner objected. They both rose to their feet. "We'll be in touch tomorrow. Kate, I'd be grateful if you talk to me before making any statement to the press. Once they get hold of this story, things are going to get messy."

Liam agreed one hundred percent. He was surprised that media trucks and reporters hadn't already descended on the house. He walked Clauson toward the door. "You're treating this as a homicide."

"Wayne Silverman has disappeared. Kate has undergone some kind of trauma. That wound on her arm appears to be from a bullet."

"Tough case," Liam said.

"You said it. I'm investigating a possible murder with no body, no weapon and no obvious motive. Oh, yeah, and the only witness has amnesia."

"Do you believe her story?"

The detective shrugged his heavy shoulders. "I got nothing else to go on."

As Clauson lumbered out of the den, Liam returned to the sofa, where Kate slouched against the plaid pillows. Her eyelids drooped.

When he sat beside her, she leaned against him. The light pressure of her slender body reminded him of how fragile and vulnerable she was. At the same time, he was aware of her femininity.

Her breast rubbed against him as she nestled against his shoulder. "I want to go home. To my house."

Liam wasn't sure it was a good idea to be isolated in a separate dwelling. "If we stay here, you ought to be safe."

"No," she said with firm decisiveness. "I didn't spend twenty-eight days hiding in the wilderness to come back and hand myself over to the people who were hunting me."

"We could arrange for a bodyguard to be posted outside your bedroom door."

She sat up straight and peered into his eyes. "I won't insult my mother like that. She'd be devastated if she thought someone in the family was threatening me. Please, Liam, take me home."

She looked exhausted and desperate, like somebody who was at the end of their rope. A dull pallor sucked the color from her tanned complexion, but she was still fighting. He respected her needs, didn't want to refuse her anything. But he also wanted her to rest. "I could talk to your mother and—"

"I've got to trust my instincts," she said. "My instincts told me to hide in the wilderness. They warned me when men were coming to your cabin."

"True."

"My instincts are telling me to go home."

"We'll go to your house."

After a predictable argument with her mother, brother and stepfather, Liam swept her out of the Carradine mansion and into his Rover. Kate's house was less than three miles away.

She sat up straight in the passenger seat, seeming to have a second wind. "Did I make a mistake in talking about Wayne's car?"

"You told the truth, didn't you?"

"As I remembered it," she said.

"Then it wasn't a mistake. Stick to the truth."

"Even when it seems improbable?"

"Always." He glanced toward her. Her fresh burst of energy reminded him of Rain, the spunky, feral woman who'd confronted him with a pistol. "You're looking wide awake."

"It's the lights," she said. "When I was in the mountains, night was dark and soft. There were animals. Mountain lions. Bears. But I felt safer there. These streetlights? They're like beacons of danger, reminding me that I can't trust anybody."

"A healthy fear is good for you, Rain. But—"

"You called me Rain."

"I meant Kate." But he didn't. Not really. The woman he cared for was Rain.

"We're here," she said.

Her house was in a cul-de-sac that butted up against a hillside. The two-story structure was white stucco, and the only hint of wilderness came from a groomed stand of aspen in her front yard.

Kate pointed the garage-door opener that was attached to the extra set of keys her mother had given her.

As the door rolled up and the garage light flashed on, Liam caught a glimpse of movement at the edge of the garage. Somebody was here. This was an ambush.

Chapter Seven

Acting on instinct, Liam reached across the bucket seats and pushed Kate down behind the dashboard. If the intruder was armed, Liam didn't want her to be a target. His first goal was to protect her.

His second goal? To catch this son of a bitch.

Liam flipped open the glove compartment, grabbed the Glock.

"What are you doing?" Kate asked.

"I saw somebody." Liam had his car door open. He ducked behind it, using the door as a shield. "I'm going after him."

No shots had been fired. And the intruder had made a run for it. "Kate, you should drive away, fast."

"Without you?"

"Just do it."

Gun in hand, Liam charged up the driveway. He rounded the edge of the garage. The glare from his headlights illuminated a narrow walkway between the garage and a chain-link fence. He spotted the figure of a man at the opposite end. Was he alone? Was he armed?

"Liam!" Kate called out to him.

He glanced back and saw her running toward him.

She'd picked a hell of a time to react with action instead of fear. "Go back to the car, Kate."

"Not unless you come with me."

Damn it, he didn't want to let this guy get away. Adrenaline pumped through his veins. His heart beat fast.

"Call nine-one-one," he yelled over his shoulder as he dived into the narrow space between the garage and a five-foot tall chain-link fence.

The mutt next door went into a barking frenzy, and the fence rattled as the dog—a big, hairy beast—crashed against the links. There ought to be a law against mastiffs in the suburbs.

In the backyard, the motion-sensitive lights had flashed on. The hillside behind her house was terraced with railroad ties in an attempt to control the wild, untamed xeriscaping that cascaded toward the edge of a redwood deck.

Liam spotted the intruder. Not a particularly difficult task. He stood in a patch of weedy-looking wildflowers, with both hands raised high above his head.

"Don't shoot," he said.

Liam scanned the rampant foliage, searching for other threats, looking for a fight. He really wanted to kick some intruder butt. But nobody else was there. He aimed the barrel of his automatic at the guy with his hands up. "Give me a reason not to pull this trigger."

"Press. I'm a reporter."

"Give me a better reason."

When Kate stepped into the backyard, the reporter's eyes popped like flashbulbs. "It's you! Kate Carradine! Oh, man, this is great. I got the scoop of the century."

She glared at him and snapped shut the cell phone. "I don't think we need the police."

"Probably not," Liam muttered. "What should I do with him?"

She stepped up beside him on the deck. "You know how I feel about trespassers."

"Right," Liam said. "Gun him down."

But he obviously couldn't shoot this idiot who was already stumbling down the hill toward them, ignoring the fact that Liam held a gun. Apparently, his journalistic instincts had overwhelmed his common sense. "My name is Mickey Wheaton, and I'm a stringer for the *Mountain Independent News*."

"I've never heard of your paper," Kate said.

"It's a weekly. Great little rag."

Liam wasn't impressed. He didn't trust the press in general, and he especially didn't trust a half-wit reporter who had been lurking around Kate's house. "What are you doing here?"

"I was listening on my police scanner and recognized the address for Kate's mother's house. I did a drive-by, saw the cop cars in front. Something was up. I took a chance that she might come here." He crowed, "And I was right. Oh, yeah!"

Mickey wore a backward Colorado Rockies cap, baggy jeans and the Vans sneakers preferred by skateboarders, but he wasn't a teenager. As he came closer, Liam guessed he was in his midtwenties, at least.

He flashed a megawatt grin. "Give me an interview, Kate."

"Not a chance," Liam answered for her.

Mickey pulled off his cap and combed his fingers through his hair in a belated attempt to look respectable. "You don't have to worry. I'm a pro. I covered Columbine and the whole JonBenet Ramsey investigation from beginning to end."

So had every other reporter in Colorado.

Mickey continued. "Kate, please. You've got to give me an exclusive."

"No, I don't."

"But it's so cool that you came back. Finally, this is a story with a happy ending. I can see the headline now." His palms raised, thumbs out at right angles to frame his invisible headline, he said, "Kate Carradine: Survivor."

Though Kate chuckled, Liam was not amused. A conversation with Mickey Wheaton could only lead to trouble.

"Come on," Mickey pleaded. "Your story could be a book deal. A bestseller. Seventeen weeks on the *Times* list."

Kate rolled her eyes. "Oh, please."

"I've studied you, Kate Carradine. I know all about your life and every detail about your disappearance. I've talked to your friends. And your enemies. By the way," he said with a grin, "if I were you, I'd keep my distance from Emily Hubbard. She still has a grudge about what happened in eighth grade."

"I broke her nose," Kate informed Liam. "It was an accident. She walked right into my tennis racket."

"Hey, I'm on your side." Mickey beamed. "You see? We're already talking like old friends. I know there's a good story behind your disappearance."

"If you know me so very well," she said, "you must be aware that the RMS publicity department will handle all press releases and stories. You should be negotiating with them. Not me."

"This is your big opportunity," Mickey said. "You can set the record straight. People think you're a spoiled little rich girl, but I know better."

"Enough," Liam said. From his time with the D.A.'s office, he knew that if there was anything more annoying than a regular reporter, it was a freelancer on the trail of a scoop. "This is the last time I ask nicely for you to leave."

Mickey sidestepped away from Liam, getting closer to Kate. "I know how much you loved your Dad. A great guy by all accounts. And I know that you felt belittled by your ex, Jonathan Proctor. And your relationship with your stepfather and mother? A little on the stormy side?" He leaned closer to her. "All in all, you have problems with men. You tend to hook up with guys who aren't good for you."

"You don't have to listen to this," Liam told her. He caught hold of the reporter's scrawny arm. "Let's go. Now."

"I'm not impressed by your pop analysis of my life," Kate said. "Tell me something I don't know."

"Your mother is missing a diamond necklace."

When she visibly winced, Liam had to wonder why. What did a missing piece of jewelry have to do with anything? Though he was curious, this wasn't an issue he intended to discuss with Mickey, who he shoved toward the garage, causing another outburst of barking from the neighbor's dog.

"Wait," she said. "Liam, could I talk to you in private for a moment?"

He dropped the reporter's arm. "Wait here, and don't move."

"You got it."

Joining Kate beside a sliding glass door at the back of her house, he asked, "What is it?"

"Mickey might be useful. If he knows all about my

disappearance, he might have details that would jog my memory."

"Bad idea," he said.

"Why?"

"The power of suggestion. He might feed you some bull that would get you thinking along the wrong line. He could divert your memory from the truth."

"Well, I'm not doing very well on my own. The only thing I could recall for Detective Clauson was about Wayne's car. And that was wrong." Kate was willing to grab at any straw. Plus, she needed to know more about the missing diamonds. "I want to talk to this guy."

"I'd rather invite a rattlesnake to tea," he grumbled. "If you really want to do this, go for it."

"Fine." She waved to Mickey, and the reporter trotted obediently toward them.

"Here's the deal," Kate said to him. "I'll talk to you if you promise not to print anything until I give the okay."

"Nothing? Not even one little sidebar article?"

"Not one word."

"Agreed," Mickey said. "We'll save it all for the book."

Liam scoffed. "As if you can trust him."

She suspected that Liam's assessment was correct; Mickey the reporter would sell her out to the highest bidder without blinking twice. "Another thing," she said. "No more sneaking around and spying. You almost got yourself shot tonight."

"Fine. And how will I contact you?"

"I'll give you my cell phone number," she said.

"Great," he said. That should keep him happy, and she could control contact on her cell.

Using her key, Kate opened the back door to her house and disengaged the alarm system. In the kitchen, she noted that her African violets had survived her absence. Everything seemed wonderfully tidy. She'd have to give the weekly cleaning lady a massive tip.

For a moment, she reveled in the joy of being surrounded by decor she'd chosen herself. The gold-streaked granite countertop. The earth-toned plates and cups displayed on open shelving. She took down a blue-tinted glass and filled it with water from the refrigerator. "Liam, Mickey, help yourselves."

Strolling through the open dining room, she smiled at the antler chandelier that hung above her table. Her mother called the pointy tines a hazard, but Kate loved the sheer, rustic goofiness of the light fixture.

In the living room were her books, her paintings, her souvenirs arranged on glass shelves. Though she'd won dozens of athletic trophies, there was only one she displayed—a small gold cup for the father-daughter relay at an RMS picnic. Kate sank into her favorite armchair, upholstered in lavender, and propped her feet on the ottoman that also served as a coffee table. Now, she felt like she was truly home.

And she couldn't help noticing that Liam fit in very nicely. His blue denim work shirt blended with the greens and purples of the sofa. His hazel eyes seemed darker. His sandy hair was the color of light oak. She liked having him here with her. A cool, masculine presence. Solid. Strong.

Mickey was the opposite. He jostled around the room like a puppet on a string. His gaze darted, no doubt recording a mental image that he could use in his proposed bestseller. A book? Kate thought not. She didn't want her life splayed across paperback pages or dribbled through the tabloids. She needed to be careful about what she said to this reporter.

Liam's low voice rumbled. "Sit, Mickey."

"Yeah, right. Okay." He perched on the edge of a chair and turned to Liam. "So, who are you? What's your connection with Kate?"

"He found me," Kate said. "Liam does volunteer work for CCC. He took some aerial photos and located the place where I was camping."

"This is even better than I thought." The reporter quivered with excitement. Again he raised his hands to frame a headline. "RMS Heiress Rescued by Pilot Stud."

"Don't even think about writing that story," Liam said.

"Come on, man. You're a macho mountain guy. I'm seeing something bigger than a book. A movie of the week. You could be played by a young Harrison Ford type."

Liam turned to Kate. "Can I throw him out now?"

"Not yet." She focused her gaze upon the scrawny, obnoxious little Mickey. "I want you to tell me every detail you've learned about my disappearance."

"Why? You were there. You ought to know."

"There are a couple of things," she said, "that I can't quite remember."

"Like what?"

"A lot of things."

He gaped, slack-jawed. His eyes widened as he figured out what she was saying. Then, his hands flew up to frame yet another headline. "Amnesia!"

"If you do that again," Liam said calmly, "I'll break both your thumbs."

"Got it," he said. "Okay, you want details. Here goes."

Kate leaned back and listened while Mickey gave a thorough description of Wayne Silverman, who could easily be lumped into the category of guys who were basically no good. A lazy, no-talent lawyer on the verge of losing the job he got through nepotism, Wayne maltreated his secretary, lived above his means and carried a lot of debt.

Preparing for his camping trip with Kate, he had strolled into an RMS store, identified himself and gotten top-of-the-line supplies for free.

"Despicable," Kate said. But she was grateful that Wayne had been an equipment snob. That gear had made her stay in the mountains a lot more comfortable.

"He told the clerk that he was going away for a week," Mickey said. "But, according to your mother's schedule—which I got from her social secretary—you were supposed to be back by Monday."

Apparently, Wayne had plans he hadn't shared with her. What other surprises were on his agenda? "Did he tell the clerk his destination?"

"Sorry," Mickey said.

"When did he depart from his town house?" she asked. "And what was he driving?"

"According to a neighbor, Wayne left around lunchtime on Friday. And he must have taken the Ford Explorer because that's the only car he owns."

"But you don't know for sure," she said. "I mean, he might have used a rental. Or borrowed an off-road vehicle from a friend."

"Is this important?" Mickey asked.

Liam cleared his throat. "Slow down, Kate. You don't have to tell him everything."

Though she would have loved verification that her memory of driving Wayne's car was correct, she agreed with Liam. This was a topic for another time. "Okay, Mickey, I have one more question and then—"

"Wait a minute! What about my questions? Like where have you been for the past twenty-eight days? Did you go to a spa? You look like you've lost a lot of weight."

"I was in the mountains," she said. "Wilderness camping."

"Alone?"

"Yes."

"What did you eat?"

"There were MREs in the backpack and I foraged. My dad taught me how to live off the land."

The little reporter was so excited that he was literally bouncing up and down in his chair. His hands flashed up for another headline. Then, he glanced at Liam and folded his arms across his chest. "Your story gets better and better, Kate. I think we're talking feature film here. Maybe starring Goldie Hawn's daughter."

"I have a question for you," Liam said. "When Kate went missing, what were the reactions from her family?"

"Her mother, Elizabeth, was very stiff-upper-lip, never giving up hope. She's a classy lady."

"And Tom?" Liam asked.

"The stepbrother. Tom Rowe." Mickey frowned as if he had some sage wisdom. "I knew Tom in high school. We weren't friends or anything, but I knew who he was. One of the cool guys."

Kate hadn't known her stepbrother during his high school years, but it surprised her that he had been one of the "in" crowd. She'd always thought of Tom as a loner.

"Did you contact Tom?" Liam asked.

"I tried. He was too busy for me."

"What about my ex, Jonathan?"

"Both Jonathan and Peter Rowe, your stepfather, played down your absence. They said you were probably off having fun and would turn up when you felt like it. Jonathan sure didn't waste any time turning your disappearance to his advantage."

"How so?" she asked.

"While you were gone, he pushed through a vote on the development of some mountain property near Cougar Creek Ski Resort. They're already putting in roads."

Though Kate was determined not make accusations until her memory returned, Jonathan was looking more and more suspicious. With her out of the way, he could turn RMS into a far more voracious corporation—taking big risks for big profits.

A yawn crept up her throat, and she realized how very tired she was. But there was one more issue. "Mickey, you mentioned something about my mother's necklace."

"I found out by accident," he said. "I was tailing your stepfather."

"Why?" she asked.

"You never know," he said mysteriously. "Anyway, Peter Rowe went into a jewelry repair shop, and I followed."

According to Mickey, Peter had taken delivery of a very impressive diamond-and-gold necklace. He and the clerk had compared it to a photograph of a piece owned by Elizabeth, then Peter had complimented the clerk on his expert work in replicating the original. When the clerk expressed a desire to see the original, Peter had said that was impossible because it was missing. "Then he corrected himself, and said it was in a bank deposit box."

Kate knew that wasn't true. Her mother kept all her valuables at the house in a fireproof safe in the den. Nobody but Elizabeth had the combination, except for the RMS attorneys who kept tabs on all family transactions.

If her mother had lost a diamond-and-gold necklace, was that the jewelry that had turned up in Kate's backpack? Though the connection would be neat and tidy, it didn't track. Her long-term memory was fairly clear. She wouldn't have forgotten such a fabulous piece of jewelry.

"Kate?" Liam called her back from her reverie.

"Sorry," she said, quickly rising to her feet. "I'm tired."

He nodded. "This interview is over, Mickey."

"But I hardly—"

"Now, Mickey."

When Liam loomed over him, Kate grinned, remembering Mickey's headline about the "Pilot Stud." Liam fit that role very well.

Before he hustled the reporter out the front door, Kate gave Mickey her cell phone number. She reset the security code when the door closed behind him. "We ought to be okay tonight," she said. "This is a fail-safe system. If anybody attempts to break in, an alarm goes off. The security company and the police are immediately alerted."

Liam seemed to relax now that the reporter was gone. He gave her an easy grin and glanced toward the staircase. "Time for bed."

Those three little words hung in the air between them. Though she knew he wasn't suggesting they go to bed together, the idea presented itself inside her head, in living color. All too vividly, she imagined what it would be like to share his bed.

In his hazel eyes, she saw a glimmer of sensual warmth. Was he thinking the same thing?

She ascended the staircase slowly. If she asked Liam to come into her bedroom, would he accept her offer? Would he hold her against his chest? His lips, she thought, would be firm and demanding. Would he taste like the forest? Would his touch transport her back to her secret mountain hideaway? Did she dare make love to him?

All these questions! She'd never been so unsure of herself. During the twenty-eight days she'd lived alone, Kate must have lost her confidence.

Or, perhaps, Liam wasn't like the other men she'd chosen.

Outside her bedroom door, Kate decided. She wasn't ready. Not tonight.

She turned to him. "The guest bedroom is across the hall, and the bathroom should be stocked with towels."

"Good night, Kate."

Alone, she entered the master bedroom. After brushing her teeth and indulging her parched skin in a quick facial scrub followed by a gallon of moisturizer, she changed into a nightshirt that hung a couple of sizes too large from her skinny shoulders. None of her wardrobe was going to fit properly until she gained back some of her weight—a problem she never thought she'd have.

Kate padded across the hardwood floor to her queen-size bed. After she'd divorced Jonathan, she'd redecorated the bedroom in a simple, austere style. The duvet and curtains were pristine white against her dark cherrywood furniture. She wriggled under the covers, enjoying the sheer luxury of Egyptian-cotton sheets. Her head was cradled by a down pillow. After weeks in the wilderness, the comfort she'd taken for granted was heavenly.

Yet, Kate was wide awake.

Her ears, accustomed to the sounds of nature, heard every creak of the floorboards. The hum from the air conditioner seemed particularly loud. She even thought she could hear the faraway hiss of traffic beyond her cul-de-sac. The neighbor's dog barked twice.

Kate flipped over to her stomach. Sleeping here should be easy. She counted backward from one hundred, concentrating on relaxation.

Still awake. Her brain leaped from topic to topic like a wayward child. The diamond necklace. Wayne Silverman's car. The purchase of equipment at an RMS outlet. Jonathan's development of the Cougar Creek property. The necklace, damn it.

She ought to tell Detective Clauson about the diamonds and cash she'd found in the backpack. The police could investigate. But what if they found the jewelry was stolen and she was the thief?

She'd tell Liam. Tomorrow. As soon as the thought crossed her mind, a pleasant calm settled over her. Liam.

She sighed. He was a good man, a trustworthy man. Surely, it was a kind fate that had led him to find her in the mountains. Thinking of him, she drifted toward sleep.

Hours later, in the buoyant flow of dreams, she heard his voice, low and gentle. She felt his nearness. His musky scent teased her nostrils. His hand was warm on her shoulder.

He whispered, "Wake up."

Her eyelids opened. In the dim light of her bedroom, she saw him leaning over her. Not a dream. Liam was here and very real.

He placed a finger across his lips, signaling silence. And she nodded, responding to the urgency in his eyes. This wasn't a playful visit. Something had gone desperately wrong.

Chapter Eight

Kate took Liam's hand, slid out from under her white duvet and went with him, leaving her dreams behind in the faint light of her bedroom. Though her brain wasn't yet in gear, she registered the fact that he was naked except for his black jersey boxer shorts. Lean like a distance runner, his muscles were well-defined but not bulging. Dark hair sprinkled across his chest and arrowed down his torso. In his left hand, he held the automatic pistol.

In the bathroom, he closed the door and didn't turn on the light. The only illumination came from a window beside the double sink. He whispered, "Someone's in the house."

"But the alarm—"

"Shhh." He motioned for her to be quiet. "I already called the cops. You stay here."

When he placed the gun in her hand, her fingers reflexively tightened on the grip, and the certainty of danger came closer.

"When I leave," he said, "lock the bathroom door. Shoot anybody who breaks in here."

"Wait," she whispered. "What are you doing?"

"I'm going after him."

His eyes were determined. Energy radiated from his tensed muscles. He looked as fierce and primitive as an ancient warrior. Invincible.

But she didn't want him to venture into danger. "Liam, no."

"I'll be okay." He picked up an aluminum baseball bat that leaned against the bathtub. "I found this in the guest bedroom."

Before she could offer further objection, he soundlessly opened the bathroom door and disappeared.

Kate locked the door, cursing the constant peril their lives had become. There was no rest. No escape. She never should have left the mountains. The hunters wouldn't give up until she was dead.

The digital clock on the windowsill read twenty-six minutes past four o'clock, the edge of dawn. She stared at the clock as another minute passed. It seemed like an hour.

The gun in her hand weighed heavily. She was supposed to protect herself. But what about Liam? He was virtually unarmed. She remembered the crude thugs who'd attacked at his cabin. If they were downstairs with their guns, Liam wouldn't stand a chance.

She couldn't allow him to go after an intruder with nothing more than naked bravery and a baseball bat. Unlocking the bathroom door, she creeped through the shadows in her bedroom.

In the upstairs hallway, she flattened herself against the wall and listened. Over the hum of the air-conditioning system, she heard the downstairs floorboards creak. Though she had thought it was impossible for anyone to bypass her fail-safe alarm system, she knew that Liam had been right—someone was here.

For an instant, she considered retreating to the bath-room again. No! She'd done enough hiding. Twenty-eight days of hiding. The only way to end this threat was to face it head-on.

Walking silently on bare feet, she went to the edge of the staircase and peeked down into the small foyer that led into the living room. Through the shadows, she saw Liam crouched inside a doorway opposite the staircase. The light from the window beside the front door shone on his baseball bat.

Another figure inched forward. He was dressed in black from head to toe. His hair was covered by a black knit cap. He wore gloves. In his hand was a pistol with a long barrel—a silencer.

Unlike the vandals who'd attacked Liam's cabin, this man knew what he was doing. He moved with cautious professional stealth across her hardwood floors. Obviously, he had taken his time in planning this assault, making sure there were no bodyguards on the lower floor of the house.

He took another step forward and lifted his chin, look-ing up the staircase. The dim light shone on his face. She didn't recognize him, but his expression was something she'd never forget—cold, dispassionate cruelty. He was a killer, a hunter. And she was his prey.

He saw her. His upper lip curled. His gun hand raised. Calmly, he took aim.

Kate froze. Terror overwhelmed her. The gun was in her hand. She needed to pull the trigger. But she couldn't move, couldn't breathe. Time stood still. In that moment, she knew she was going to die.

Liam lashed out with his bat.

But the dark intruder had sensed the attack and side-stepped. He pivoted.

Liam charged and swung again.

She heard the clank of the aluminum bat striking the metal of the gun. There was a huffing noise and a pop as a bullet buried itself in her hardwood floor. The intruder retreated, heading back toward the kitchen.

Liam followed. Was he crazy? With a baseball bat, he was going up against a professional assassin. If anything happened to this wonderful, brave, idiotic man, she'd never forgive herself.

Belatedly, she raced down the staircase and ran toward the living room.

Liam caught her around the waist and pulled her against his chest. His back was to the wall. "I told you to stay upstairs."

"I'm here now."

"Damn it, Kate."

They heard the back door crash open.

"Hurry," she said. "He's getting away."

"Let him go," Liam said.

"Why?"

"I'd guarantee that he's a better shot than you or I. If it came to a showdown, he'd win."

In response to the back door being open, her security alarm screeched. At the same time, police sirens echoed from the street. The dog next door set up a howl.

Only minutes ago, she'd been sleeping. Now, Kate stood in the midst of a nightmare. The discordant noises crashed against her eardrums and ricocheted inside her head. Her nerves were strung tight as piano wire; one more twist and she would surely snap.

Liam's arms closed protectively around her, and she leaned her back against his chest.

"He's gone," Liam said. "You're safe."

"I should have shot him." She shivered in his arms. Only the thin fabric of her nightshirt separated his flesh from hers. "He was standing right there. I missed my chance."

"The important thing is that you're all right."

"And you." With her left hand, she stroked the crisp hair on his forearm. For one brief instant, the connection between them was something more than friendship. She was utterly aware of their intimacy, and she wanted it to be more. She wanted him to be aware of her as a woman, as desirable.

Clearly, this wasn't the right time. The police were banging at the front door, and the alarm continued to scream.

Liam gave her a squeeze, then released her. "You've got to turn off that damn alarm."

She stumbled toward the keypad and plugged in the code as Liam went to answer the front door. For a moment, she was distracted by his near-naked body, perfectly proportioned from his shoulders to his heels. His back tapered to a lean torso and a tight butt. When he excused himself to go upstairs to put on clothes, she decided that it was a terrible shame to cover that body.

Two uniformed cops—a man and a woman—came toward her. Kate led them into the kitchen, where she found a month-old container of coffee and made a pot. Before it had brewed, Liam was back downstairs, fully clad.

Another patrol car arrived. More policemen were in her house. Though there were only five of them, they seemed like a crowd of huge, armed people in uniforms, all of whom were asking questions.

Yes, she told them, there were several other people who had keys to her house. Her mother, obviously. Her cleaning lady. Her ex-husband.

Yes, these people also knew the codes to the alarm system.

No, she didn't recognize the intruder.

No, she didn't know why an armed assassin would be after her. She only knew it was true. Someone wanted her dead.

The questions continued. The police roamed through her house, peering into corners. She didn't want them here. She wanted to be left alone.

Liam slipped his arm around her waist. "That's enough," he told the cops. "I'm taking her upstairs to bed."

Over their objections, he whisked her up the staircase and into her bedroom, where he closed the door.

Crossing the room, she turned on the bedside lamp. Compared to downstairs, it was quiet here—creating the impression of a peaceful, safe haven. But it was only an illusion, a pipe dream. "I won't be able to sleep."

"Have you got a suitcase?"

"Of course."

"Throw some clothes in it. We're getting out of here."

She perched on the edge of her unmade bed. "Can we do that?"

He sat beside her and crossed his legs. His right ankle rested on his left knee. He was barefoot. His long, narrow foot was pale and perfect, like a da Vinci sketch of the human anatomy.

"This is what's happening," he said. "That guy who came into your house was a pro."

She nodded agreement. "A hired killer."

"And he didn't break in. He had a key. And he knew the code to disarm the security system. That means he was sent by someone in your family."

With a mental thud, the pieces fell into place. Her suspicions about her family were confirmed. And she couldn't keep it a secret much longer. Detective Clauson would surely come to the same conclusion as Liam had.

The situation was about to get very uncomfortable.

Liam continued. "As long as they know where you are, it's not safe."

"Where will we go?"

"There's a guy in town who owes me a favor from when I was with the D.A.'s office. He runs a little motel. Nothing fancy. But I figure that works to our advantage. Nobody will look for Kate Carradine, the RMS heiress, at a plain little mom-and-pop motel."

She grabbed the jeans that belonged to his nephew and slipped into them. "Let's go."

"Don't you need other clothes?"

She plucked at the baggy folds of her nightshirt. "Everything I own is two or three sizes too big."

"Got a sweatshirt with a hood?"

"No prob."

The inside of her walk-in closet clearly showed the two sides of her personality. An array of sweatshirts, team jerseys, ski clothes and hiking gear covered one wall. The other was business suits, respectable dresses and formal gowns in dry cleaner's bags. She grabbed a hooded maroon sweatshirt and slipped her feet into running shoes.

Liam had followed her. He pulled out a clear plastic bag containing a long, scarlet sheath. "Pretty."

"RMS sponsors a lot of charity events." Kate didn't know why she should feel defensive, but she did. "It's my job to attend them."

The weight of the red fabric slipped through his fingers. "Something like this would look good with a diamond necklace."

"But I don't own one."

"Your mother might let you wear hers. The one Peter made a copy of." Liam crossed the small space, trapping her against her clothes. "You know something about that necklace, don't you?"

Kate said nothing. She needed to tell him about the jewels and cash she'd found in the backpack. But not now. Not while the downstairs of her house swarmed with cops. "It's complicated. My memories are all jumbled up."

"No more secrets, Kate. It's too dangerous."

The attack by the professional assassin had made it clear to Liam that they needed to find answers. Fast. Whoever was after Kate wasn't wasting time. The only way to keep her safe was to find the truth buried in her shaky memory.

Tension pinched her forehead. "I want to get away from here."

He tried to make sense of her reluctance. "Are you protecting someone? Your mother?"

"My mother has nothing to do with this," she snapped. "She's been through enough. The death of my father nearly destroyed her."

Kate walked out of the closet and went to the bedroom door. "Please, let's get away from here so I can think."

AFTER CLAUSON ARRIVED, Liam negotiated a quick getaway. The police would stay at Kate's house, working up the forensics in case the gloved intruder had left behind any clues—fibers, footprints, any trace of his identity.

Liam would take Kate to an undisclosed location, and

he promised to stay in touch via cell phone. When they drove away from her house, dawn colored the sky with pink and yellow streaks. The weather report on the car radio promised another warm, clear August day along the front range.

Before they went to the motel, he drove to a diner on Colfax. Liam zipped into the parking lot and parked between two trucks. "You'll like this place," he promised. "Best Denver omelet in town."

She hopped out of the car before he had a chance to open the door for her. "Is it safe? Should we just waltz into a restaurant?"

"This isn't the kind of place where anybody would expect to find Kate Carradine."

"I don't know why you keep saying things like that. When you first saw me, I looked like Granny Clampett. I hadn't bathed or washed my hair in a month. My pants were held up with twine."

And he'd thought she was beautiful. Like a wood nymph, she was natural, unaffected. The essence of that feral woman who called herself Rain still beckoned to him.

But the woman who sat in the leatherette booth across from him was Kate Carradine. Her net worth was in the millions. In her closet, she had ball gowns with shoes dyed to match. He would never be a part of that world. He didn't *want* to apply for membership in that country club.

After they both ordered the Denver omelet, her gaze focused on the television perched on a high stand in the corner of the diner. The sound was on low as the morning news team gave a traffic report. Kate watched, mesmerized. "It's been a while since I've seen television. It's kind of magical."

He watched the flickering change of expressions across her face. Her tanned skin pulled tight across her high cheekbones. The dark hollows beneath her eyes showed a need for sleep and nourishment. It was obvious to him that she needed rest, and it wouldn't do him any good to push her for answers. Not right at this moment. "I'll never understand you, Kate."

"Why?"

"You're a walking contradiction. One minute, you're excited by a television set. The next, you're talking about the need to attend charity balls."

"My family's rich," she said. "That doesn't mean I'm a snob."

"The family mansion threw me off. And your mother's live-in cook. Your own weekly maid service. And wasn't that a brand new Beemer I saw parked inside your garage?"

"It's nice to have beautiful things. Even nicer when my money can make a difference."

"How so?"

"As soon as this is over, I'm going to concentrate on that mountain camp for disadvantaged kids. With my real-life foraging experience, I can teach them an important lesson."

Her eyes brightened. As she talked about her plans for the mountain camp, he saw the better side of Kate. "And what's the most important lesson?"

"Living off the land," she said. "You don't need money. You don't need cars or fancy clothes. Everything you need is right there in front of your eyes. The natural resources. Use what you have."

He nodded, sharing her opinion. "I like the way you think."

She gave him an almost carefree grin. "I might be an heiress, but I'm also a typical woman. A lot of those things Mickey said about me were true."

"I don't trust that little weasel," Liam said. "I wasn't really paying attention to what he said."

"I'll remind you. Pop psychology. Mickey said my judgment in men is lousy. And he was right on target. I always fall for the wrong guy. From Jonathan the jerk to Wayne the…"

"The missing?" he said.

Her blue eyes turned dark. He'd noticed that when she was upset or worried, her jaw tightened as though she were clenching her teeth. "If only I could remember. Why did I agree to go away with him for the weekend?"

"For kicks?"

"It's possible, but he sounds like a total sleazeball—mistreating his secretary, demanding freebies from the RMS outlet. Maybe I was going out with him to tick off my mother." She groaned. "God, that sounds like a spoiled little rich girl."

"Another contradiction."

As she gazed across the table at him, her eyebrow lifted. She seemed to be assessing him. "I'm kind of attracted to you, Liam. And you seem normal. Is there something you're not telling me?"

"Like the dancing squirrels at my cabin," he said, teasing. "Every full moon, they do a chorus line. 'Puttin' on the Ritz.'"

The look she gave him was uncertain. "Not really."

"And then, there was the time I got abducted by aliens. Long-necked chameleon people who could shape-shift."

"Stop it."

"They're here among us." He looked directly at her

and crossed his eyes. "George Washington was actually from planet Nebulus."

"Idiot!"

It was good to see her laugh. He actually felt a warmth growing inside his chest. Heartwarming? Liam had always thought that was only a metaphor.

As quick as her chuckle, Kate's hand flew to cover her mouth. Looking alarmed, she stared up at the corner television.

He turned his head. On the screen was her stepfather, Peter Rowe, standing outside the Carradine mansion and speaking into a microphone.

Liam rose and turned up the audio.

"…and so, her mother and I are very grateful," Peter said. "Kate's resting, but I'm sure she'll be happy to give a statement when she's able. Her health appears to be good, but we will have her examined by a doctor and a psychiatrist."

"A shrink?" Kate said under her breath. "Does he think I'm crazy?"

As if responding to her question, Peter elaborated for the news reporter. "Kate isn't emotionally disturbed, unless you count her legendary temper." He put on his charming, Robert Wagner smile. "But she seems to be suffering from some sort of paranoid delusion."

"Delusion?" she said angrily.

"However," Peter said, "we're certain that she'll be fine. Her mother and I are happy to have our daughter home."

The photograph of Kate with her pearl necklace flashed on the screen behind the news anchor, who concluded, "We will provide updates on the rescue of Kate Carradine, who was missing in the mountains for twenty-eight days."

Liam adjusted the sound and returned to the table as the omelets arrived.

"This is just swell," Kate hissed. "Peachy! My stepfather is telling the whole world that I'm a candidate for the loony bin."

Liam took a bite of his omelet.

She continued. "A paranoid delusion? Were those thugs who shot up your plane a delusion? And the professional assassin last night?"

"Peter's a jerk. You're not the only one in your family with bad judgment about men."

"You're so right. Mom never should have married him."

He nodded toward the fluffy eggs with ham, cheese and green peppers. "Eat before it gets cold."

"Right." She dug in with her fork. "I want to be at full strength when I strangle Peter Rowe."

Chapter Nine

The more Kate thought about Peter Rowe, the angrier she got. Her temper simmered all the way through breakfast, during the drive along Colfax Avenue and after they had checked into the no-frills motel that belonged to Liam's friend.

While Liam went to park his car behind the motel so it wouldn't be seen, she stalked around the small room, which was simple and clean with a TV, a dresser and side-by-side double beds. It was definitely not the sort of five-star hotel where she usually stayed. Room service was probably the burger joint across the parking lot. But the lack of amenities had nothing to do with her anger.

Nothing about this situation was fair. She'd been attacked twice and driven from her home. The final straw was being slandered by her stepfather on the morning news.

Pacing the worn path in the carpet, her outrage spiked higher. She knew, rationally, that tantrums didn't solve anything. They were selfish, and she always felt guilty after a blowup. It was preferable to remain in control. But how?

Her fingers clenched around the top of the low wood

chair in front of the desk, and she held on tight, wishing for the depth and clarity of purpose she'd had when she was Rain.

In the mountains, her priority had been clear: survival. Nothing else had mattered. In the mountains, when she'd felt rage, she'd expressed herself with a burst of wild, uncontrolled sobbing or a primal scream that sent the jays and sparrows soaring into the skies like darts.

Here, in civilization, those natural responses would surely get her committed to an insane asylum.

Liam returned to the room. When he glanced toward her, she saw a hint of antipathy; he was irritated with her mood. And wasn't that just too damn bad!

Without a word, he pulled the drapes closed, nearly blocking out the morning light, and adjusted the air-conditioning, causing the fan to emit an annoying rattle. Then he turned down the garishly patterned bedspread and patted the pillow. "Here you go," he said. "Time to catch up on your sleep."

"I'm not tired," she snapped.

"You got less than six hours last night," he said.

"What are you? My mother?" She hated the sound of her own voice—cranky, annoyed and more than a little bitchy.

His jaw tightened, but he didn't respond to her snit. His attitude remained calm. Excessively calm. "You've put your body through a lot in the past month. You need to rest, to prepare for the coming stress."

"What stress?"

"When you go public, all hell will break loose."

"I don't care."

"You should," he said.

"Don't tell me what I should and shouldn't do."

Though she didn't want to lash out at him, the pressure was building. Her fingers tightened into fists. "I'm sick of hiding, Liam. I hate being so helpless, waiting around for the next attack. I want to do something. Anything! Isn't there some kind of action we can take?"

"Not until you remember what happened."

"As if I have a choice?" Damn it, he didn't understand anything. "Are you insinuating that I'm purposely forgetting?"

He lifted one accusing eyebrow. "You haven't told me all the details."

Some things she couldn't reveal. Not about the cash and the jewelry. Not about her vision of a man who had been shot. Not until she knew what they meant. "Some of my memories are none of your business."

"You're afraid to talk."

Her grip on self-control stretched to the limit. "How dare you accuse me of being scared!"

"Then tell me," he said.

"I don't remember."

"The hell you don't."

She charged at him, got right up in his face. Her forefinger jabbed at his chest. "This isn't my fault."

He clamped hold of her wrist and held on tight. There were flames behind his eyes, but his tone was cool. "This must be the legendary Kate Carradine temper."

"Damn straight."

"I'm not impressed."

She tried to yank free from his grasp, but he held her wrist in a firm, unshakable grip. Glaring, she said, "You don't know what's best for me. You don't know what I want."

"You want your own way," he said. "And you're mad as hell."

"I have every right to be angry. Peter's telling the world that I'm nuts. Assassins are breaking into my house."

"You're right." His face had never been so serious. "You're in mortal danger. Somebody's trying to kill you."

His words bored into her consciousness like a molten poker, stirring the flames. Unbearable heat welled up inside her. She could feel her face turning red. "I don't want to— I can't think about it."

"You're scared," he said. "And you have valid reasons for your fear. That's why you're mad. That's what you don't want to face."

She struggled against his superior strength. Frustration fed her temper. "Let go of me."

"You want to yell," he said. "You want to throw things and kick holes in the wall. Go ahead. Do it."

"No!" She fought the rising tide within her.

"It's not anger, Kate. It's never been anger. It's fear."

"I can't—" Her entire body clenched in a painful knot. Breathing hard, a scream crawled up her throat, but the sound that left her lips was a groan—a gut-wrenching, long, sustained groan, as if she were lifting a weight of five hundred pounds.

She thrashed, whimpered and groaned again. Her lungs felt like they would explode.

"Breathe," Liam said.

And she did.

"Slowly," he added.

The intake of oxygen eased the tension that gripped her rib cage in an iron vise. In a gasp, she inhaled again. Again.

The clenched, burning sensation began to fade. Tension snapped; her muscles went loose. When Liam released her wrists, her knees folded and she sank down on the bed. Her shoulders slumped forward.

He patted her back, and she recoiled. Then, she relaxed and accepted his touch. Her body ached, and she suddenly felt exhausted. "I didn't mean for that to happen."

"It's over," he said.

"I behaved badly."

Gently, he lifted her chin and gazed into her eyes. Though she'd accused him of being callous, Kate had been wrong. From the way he looked at her, she knew he understood her rage and her fear. The depth of his comprehension startled her. Somehow, he had gotten inside her and exorcised the demon.

A tentative grin lifted the corners of his mouth. "You need rest."

"I know." With a surprising lack of effort, she smiled back at him. A moment ago, a smile was a million miles away. He was a miracle worker.

"Know how I can tell you're tired?" he asked. "By the rings under your eyes."

"Is that like telling the age of a tree by counting the rings?"

"You bet." He ran his thumbs across the skin below her eyes. "I'd say two, maybe three, more hours of sleep are called for."

Placing both his hands on her shoulders, he lowered her onto the pillows. Weakly, Kate protested, "It doesn't seem right to sleep."

He stepped back and sat on the other bed. "What else do you have in mind?"

"I want to respond to Peter's comment about my paranoid delusions."

"You want to contact the press?"

Not really. Though she regularly dealt with the media when she publicized RMS events, this was different. The cameras would focus directly on her, probing her behavior, questioning her decision to hide. And what could she tell them? *I don't remember. I might be a thief. Maybe I shot somebody.*

If she showed up in her ragamuffin clothes with hair sticking out in all directions, the reporters would know for sure that she was a loon. "For right now, I should call my mother and tell her to put a muzzle on Peter."

"There's a plan," Liam said. "Don't give her our location."

He handed her the cell phone from her purse, and she turned it on. There were three calls from Mickey, but now was not the time to answer them. She punched in the number for her mother.

On the third ring, Elizabeth answered. "Kate, darling. I heard about what happened at your house. Are you all right?"

"I'm okay."

"I told you not to go to your own place," her mother reprimanded. "If you had stayed here last night…"

Kate listened with half attention as her mother rambled on, talking about the intensive security at the Carradine mansion. Unfortunately, Mom didn't understand the real problem. Kate didn't need protecting from outsiders; she was under attack from someone within the family circle.

Her mother concluded, "Where are you?"

"Somewhere safe. I'm with Liam."

"You know I don't like to interfere in your life," Elizabeth said. "But I don't think it's wise to get involved with that young man."

"Why not?"

Kate watched Liam as he stretched out on the other bed. He was deep into his own cell phone conversation. His baritone voice played an unintentional counterpoint to her mother's high soprano. Getting involved with him was possibly the smartest decision she could make.

She cut into her mother's standard listing of reasons why she ought to be careful about the men she dated. "I need to ask a favor, Mom."

"Anything, dear."

"None of my clothes fit. Could you arrange to get me two outfits? I'll pick them up. One dressy, like a suit. One casual. A couple of sizes smaller than usual."

"Certainly." Sheer delight rippled through her mother's voice. Elizabeth adored shopping. "Anything else?"

"I saw Peter on television, and I don't appreciate his comments about my sanity, or the lack thereof."

"He's trying to do the best thing for you," Elizabeth said, automatically defending her creepy husband. "We think a psychiatrist might be able to help with your little amnesia problem."

"That's entirely possible," Kate said. Now that her rage had passed, she was willing to be reasonable. "But we don't really need to announce to the media that I've gone completely off my rocker, do we?"

"I suppose Peter might have said a bit too much."

"A bit." He'd practically been waving a straitjacket in his hand. "I'll see you later, Mom."

"Be careful, dear."

Disconnecting the call, Kate turned her cell phone off. After slipping out of her jeans and shoes, she got under the covers. The motel bed was too hard and the sheets were rough, not at all like the Egyptian cotton at her house, but she wouldn't complain. It was fabulous to have any bed at all.

A soothing wave of exhaustion washed over her. At breakfast, she'd managed to eat more than half of her omelet, and her stomach felt comfortably full. She was glad to be here, glad to be alive, especially glad that she'd finally found a man who understood her legendary temper and accepted her anyway.

LIAM HADN'T INTENDED TO sleep at the motel. His plan was to put together all the facts he'd learned so far and come up with a theory of why someone wanted Kate dead. The next time someone came after her, he'd know who and why. If he could figure this out, maybe there wouldn't be a next time.

But the facts were scarce, and the conclusion was much too obvious. Before Kate had gone into hiding, she'd witnessed something. A murder? A theft? Arson? If her memory came back, she could finger the guilty party. Therefore, the criminal wanted her dead.

The only way Liam would get answers was if Kate started remembering. He glanced over at the other bed. She was already asleep, her breathing slow and steady. She looked peaceful, almost sweet. Quite a contrast to the screeching harpy who'd jabbed her finger at his chest.

That anger was a part of her, not necessarily a negative. He knew that her rage masked an even deeper fear and gave her the strength to fight. She'd managed to survive on sheer guts, and he had to respect that.

They had come a distance toward understanding each other, but not far enough. She still didn't trust him enough to tell all her secrets.

He stretched out on the bed and closed his eyes.

When he woke, it was almost noon. On the other bed, Kate slept fitfully. The back of her hand rubbed against her cheek like a cat cleaning its whiskers. She exhaled a soft sigh and rolled onto her side, facing him. Her eyelids fluttered open.

"Hi," she murmured.

"Hi, yourself."

"You were right. Sleep was good."

Good enough for her to start trusting him? "Kate, we need to talk. I want you to tell me everything. Every detail."

She buried her face in the pillow. "I'd rather sleep some more."

"The sooner we figure out who's trying to kill you, the sooner this will be over."

As she stretched and yawned, he was again reminded of a cat—a standoffish creature who went her own way and expected to be catered to. She wiggled around under the covers until she was sitting up.

"We'll talk," she said. "You first."

"When Mickey mentioned that necklace, you knew what he was referring—"

"No, no, no," she interrupted. "I don't want to talk about me. I'm sick to death of me. Tell me something about yourself."

"Like what?"

"I told you that my problem in relationships was bad judgment," she said. "What's yours?"

"I don't have a problem."

She lifted a skeptical eyebrow. "You're in your thirties, not married and living alone in the mountains. Why?"

This wasn't a conversation he wanted to have. "My solitary status doesn't have anything to do with why somebody keeps trying to kill you. It's no big secret why I live alone. I haven't found the right woman."

"What are you looking for?"

"You've seen my cabin. My lifestyle is all about peace and quiet. Not a lot of action. No shopping malls." He swung his legs over the edge of the bed and sat facing her. "I'm looking for a woman who wouldn't be bored in a log cabin on a rainy day."

She mimicked his action. Her knees were inches away from his. "Rain," she said.

"Beautiful Rain." He looked into her face and saw the spirited woman who'd lived in the forest and spent her days weaving baskets of twigs. Rain. Moist and soft and refreshing.

Liam forgot about his questions and the threat of danger. For a moment, he lost himself in the blue depths of her eyes. She could be the woman he'd been looking for, the woman who would share his cabin and his life.

As he leaned closer toward her, she glanced away. Her gaze rested on the bedside clock. "Oh my God," she said. "It's noon. We ought to watch the news."

She bounced off the bed, grabbed the remote and turned on the television in time to hear the midday anchor say, "For new information on the rescue of Kate Carradine, we're going live to the Carradine mansion west of Denver."

Kate glanced over her shoulder at Liam. "My mother promised me that she wouldn't allow Peter to talk."

The man on the television screen wasn't Peter Rowe. This guy appeared to be Liam's age. He was smooth, almost sculpted. His formal attitude made his casual shirt and tie look like a three-piece suit.

"Jonathan," Kate said.

So, this was her ex-husband, the CEO of RMS. Liam had a hard time reconciling Kate—who was vivacious and bright—with this cold, monochromatic man.

"Last night," he said, speaking directly into the camera, "an intruder entered Kate's home. We don't believe this was a coincidence."

The reporter asked for his conclusions, and Jonathan replied, "This is speculation on my part. Kate was missing for nearly a month. Surely, she couldn't have survived on her own."

"Did, too," she snapped at the television.

"Therefore," her ex-husband continued, "we believe it's possible that she was abducted and held prisoner."

The news reporter asked, "Could this have been part of a terrorist plot?"

He frowned, seeming to give serious consideration to the idea. "Difficult to say."

"So, you suspect terrorism?"

"I don't rule out any possibility."

When asked about ransom demands, he was huffy. "Certainly not. If we had received demands, we would have taken the appropriate steps."

Kate whirled to face Liam. "Do you believe this?"

He couldn't believe she had actually been married to this jerk. Sure, the guy wasn't bad-looking, but he was a stiff. Self-important. Without any discernible personality.

Then the camera focused on Peter Rowe. Tom stood right beside him, shuffling his feet and looking uncomfortable under the lights.

"Oh, no," Kate said.

Peter tossed a winning smile at the camera and said,

"I don't agree with Jonathan. Kate's mother and I are convinced that she's suffering from paranoid delusions or maybe post-traumatic stress disorder."

The next face on the screen was the news reporter on the scene, who summarized, "There you have two opinions on what happened to Kate Carradine during the twenty-eight days she was missing. The real question is—when will we hear from the lady herself?"

"Real soon," Kate said. She was already putting on her jeans. "Whether I like it or not, I have to set these people straight."

Liam didn't agree. Though it couldn't be fun for her to listen to these two idiots speculating on what was wrong with her, Jonathan and Peter made a good distraction. "You're better off here, Kate."

"While the whole city thinks I've been kidnapped by terrorists?" She shook her head in utter disbelief. "What a bizarre concept! RMS is basically a sporting-goods wholesaler. Does Jonathan think terrorists are plotting to steal the latest design in tennis rackets?"

Liam shrugged. "RMS carries guns."

"Hunting rifles," she said. "We also handle starter pistols, flare guns and crossbows. Somehow, I doubt that the terrorist armies want to be equipped with crossbows."

"Hey, I'm not defending your ex-husband."

"I certainly hope not."

"But I am suggesting that you take a step back and leave Jonathan and Peter in the limelight. The less attention on you, the better."

"Maybe you're right."

"Do you really care what other people think?" Liam asked. "Is public opinion important to you?"

"If you'd asked me that a month ago, I would have said

yes. But now?" She grinned. "Other people's opinions don't matter."

"Truth is all that matters," he said.

"Unfortunately, I can't remember the whole truth."

She'd left open the door to his questions. What hadn't she told him? What was she keeping a secret? Before Liam could phrase his questions, he heard the screech of brakes in the motel parking lot.

Quickly, he went to the curtain and pulled it aside. A television news truck barreled toward their room. Another two cars followed. "Looks like you're not going to have a choice about meeting the press. They're here."

"How did they find us?"

"Somebody must have recognized you from the televised reports and called them."

If given a choice between being attacked by a professional assassin and facing a local news team, Liam wasn't sure which alternative he'd pick. With an assassin he at least had a chance of getting away. Or dying quick. Which seemed preferable to being hounded to death by a persistent reporter.

He motioned for Kate to join him in the bathroom, where he cranked open the casement window. Even with the window open to the max, the space was narrow. He wouldn't fit through. But Kate would.

"Go ahead," he said. "You first."

She raised a skeptical eyebrow. "You want me to climb out the window and run away?"

"Basically."

"Why?" she asked.

Because he still had unanswered questions about her memories. Because he wanted to avoid the inevitable scrutiny of publicity. "Because there isn't time for discussion. Just do it."

"Climb out the bathroom window?"

He could already hear the pounding on the motel room door. "You go out the window, get in my car and bring it around to the front. I'll meet you."

She shrugged. "And everybody thinks I'm the crazy person."

She allowed him to boost her up to the sill. It was a tight squeeze, even for her slender body. When she was safely outside, he tossed her the car keys. "Two minutes," he said. "Out in front."

Liam went to answer the door. A trim, blond reporter stood waiting with microphone in hand. Behind her, a cameraman focused on the door.

"Liam MacKenzie," she said. "I remember you from the D.A.'s office."

"Joyce." He recognized her, and he knew that her gleaming white smile masked the appetite of a barracuda when she was after a story. A few years back, when he'd prosecuted a high-profile murder case, she'd stalked him, gone through his garbage and tried to plant a bug in his car.

"You're back in the news," she said cheerfully. "You found Kate Carradine. Want to tell me about it?"

He said nothing. Not one sound bite.

Joyce craned her neck, trying to see around him. "Is she here? Kate?"

"She's in the bathroom, tidying up. Come inside and you can wait."

He held the door wide for Joyce and her cameraman. As they entered, he left. Dodging around a second reporter, Liam spotted his car. He leaped into the passenger seat. "Go."

Chapter Ten

Liam was thrown back against the passenger seat of the
Land Rover as Kate peeled out of the parking lot and onto
the street.

"Buckle up," she warned.

"Just go." Peering through the rear window, he saw the
reporters scrambling for their trucks.

Kate left them in the dust. Behind the wheel, she was
fast but safe, negotiating her way across traffic for a quick
left turn onto a busier street. She dodged onto a side road,
then another and another until she hit a deserted two-lane.

Then she floored it. He'd never known his Rover could
move like this. After a couple of blocks, she whipped a
one-eighty and drove back in the direction they'd come
from, making sure nobody was following.

"Where did you learn how to drive?" he asked.

"Driving is a sport, and I'm good at sports. Besides,
RMS is one of the sponsors for the Grand Prix of Den-
ver," she said. "I had a couple of lessons from the pros.
Where are we headed?"

Though he was tempted to tell her to point west and
keep driving into the mountains, Liam knew there was
no escape from the press. "You're going to have to make

a statement, sooner or later. It's your choice on where you do it."

"My mother's house," she said decisively. "She promised to get me some clothes. If I have to face the media, I want to look decent."

Liam figured they were only half an hour away from the Carradine mansion. Once they got there, their privacy would be shot. Kate would be swept up in a whirlwind of reporters, doctors and her family—one of whom was probably trying to kill her.

"It's time, Kate. You've got to tell me the details you've been holding back."

Her slender fingers tightened on the steering wheel. Her lips compressed into a tight line, and he thought she was planning to stonewall him. Again.

Then she spoke. "In my memory, I saw a man. Could have been Wayne Silverman or someone else. I don't know. I wasn't looking at his face. His chest was covered with blood. So much blood. He'd been shot."

"Murder." Liam had suspected as much. "You witnessed a murder. Now the killer wants you out of the way."

She darted a glance toward him. "I want to believe that's what happened. That I was a witness."

"Why would you doubt it?"

"I was afraid." He saw the tension around her eyes and jaw. Her lips drew back from her teeth as she forced the words through them. "I was afraid that I might have killed him."

Finally, he understood her reluctance to tell him everything. Because she couldn't remember the whole scene, she was afraid of what she might have done. "Believe me, Kate, you're not a murderer. Even when you were face-to-face with that intruder in your house, you couldn't pull the trigger."

"But how can I know for sure?"

"I know," he said firmly. "I've dealt with killers, and that's not you."

He carefully avoided mentioning the possibility that she might have fired the gun in self-defense or by accident. Experience had taught him that innocent people were capable of murder when threatened.

"All the same," she said. "You can see why I don't want to tell Detective Clauson about this. Not until I have a clearer picture."

"No problem. I think Clauson is assuming murder, anyway." They were rapidly approaching the turnoff that led to her mother's house, and he didn't have time to waste on subtlety. "What about the diamond necklace?"

"I'm not sure what it means."

"Tell me what you know, and do it fast. When you step back into your mother's house, we won't be able to talk."

Her eyes widened in alarm. "You're not going to leave me there alone, are you?"

"I'll be there." He reached over and rested his hand on her shoulder. Though she was rail-thin beneath the baggy sweatshirt, there was no question about her femininity. Kate was all woman, and when she met his gaze, he saw the promise of sensuality in the lift of her eyebrow and the tilt of her chin.

Liam had intended for his touch to reassure her, but their slight physical contact had a more potent effect on him. All these little pats and hugs were piling up, creating a tension that begged for release.

"About the necklace," she said. "It isn't a memory. It's a fact. Again, it looks bad for me."

"Go on."

"When I woke up in the meadow, my mind was blank. All I had was the backpack—Wayne's backpack—full of supplies from RMS."

Cranking the steering wheel, she whipped a right, avoiding the slowdown for construction on a side street.

She continued. "The backpack contained more than camping gear. There was cash. I found thousands of dollars in neat bundles of hundreds. And a pouch of jewelry. Gold and diamonds."

He blinked. This revelation was totally unexpected. "You have no idea where it came from?"

"None," she said.

When they had left her campsite, they'd brought the backpack with them. He remembered carrying it from the plane to his cabin. "What did you do with the loot?"

"I hid it in my cave," she said. "I was afraid. Liam, what if I stole those things? What if Wayne and I were making a getaway?"

"Why would you steal your mother's necklace?"

"I can't remember if the diamonds belong to Elizabeth. The necklace didn't look familiar, and I didn't recognize the design."

"It might be new," he said.

"It wasn't until Mickey talked about Peter making a copy that I thought it might belong to my mother."

Which still didn't answer Liam's question. "Why steal from your own mother?"

"I don't know. Maybe I was trying to get back at her. Maybe I was angry."

"The legendary Kate Carradine temper."

But he still couldn't believe she'd go to all that trouble to snatch her mom's jewelry. Kate didn't need the money. Since she couldn't even recall what the necklace looked like, she hadn't taken it for sentimental reasons.

"I'd like to think I wasn't such a brat," she said. "So, here's a different theory. Nobody has the combination to the safe in the library where Mom keeps her valuables except for her and the family attorney—that's the firm where Wayne works."

"You're thinking that Wayne got hold of the combination and swiped the necklace." Liam saw a hole in that theory. "Why would he take the necklace on your camping trip? Was he making a getaway?"

"Maybe," she said.

"If so, why did he take you along?"

"It doesn't make sense," she said miserably. "Not unless I knew his plans. Not unless I'm a thief."

She was approaching her mother's house. "Pull over," he said.

She glided to the curb and parked in front of an attractively landscaped yard. This housing development had obviously grown up around the sprawling Carradine property near the foothills. These were nice, new homes in neutral colors. Organized and tidy, they were in direct contrast to the chaotic speculation inside Liam's head.

The worst-case scenario: Kate was a murderer and a thief. She and Silverman had stolen the necklace. Then she'd killed him.

More likely, she was guilty of bad judgment—aiding and abetting Wayne Silverman.

"How much cash?" he asked.

"It was fifty thousand when I found it. All in hundreds. But I used some."

"In the mountains? How did you use it?"

"For kindling," she said.

She had been burning hundred-dollar bills. While scraping out the barest nourishment for survival, she still managed to be extravagant. A woman of many contradictions.

He stared into her wide blue eyes—the innocent color of periwinkle sparkled with a laser edge. If he reached out to stroke her cheek, she might bite his finger off. Or she might kiss his hand. Unpredictable as the Colorado weather, she intrigued him. At the same time, she drove him crazy. "You always keep me guessing."

"I want to know the truth as much as you do."

"Is there anything else you haven't told me?"

"That's everything I remember. The blood. The jewels. The forest fire. Driving Wayne's car. And the hunters coming after me."

A veritable kaleidoscope of clues. There had to be a connection, but Liam couldn't see it. Instead, his gaze lingered on her trusting smile. She felt close enough to tell him her secrets.

The questions he wanted to ask at this moment had nothing to do with solving a murder. He wanted to know how it felt to hold her in his arms all night. He wanted to taste the morning dew on her lips. To make love to her. To discover the secrets of her body and her heart.

"Here's another glitch in my theory," she said, "about Wayne being the thief."

He tried to drag his attention back to the crime. "A glitch?"

"The money and the jewels were probably worth a hundred and fifty to two hundred thousand. I don't think Wayne Silverman would throw away his career for that amount."

"People have killed and been killed for a lot less. He might have been desperate."

"Why?"

"Gambling debt, blackmail, embezzlement. Wayne specialized in legal audits. That leaves a lot of room for white-collar crime." He shrugged and tore his gaze away from her. "We need to know more about Wayne Silverman. I'll put in a call to Molly at CCC."

Kate rubbed her palms together. "This is starting to sound like a plan."

"There's something else we need to do. As soon as possible."

She looked expectantly toward him. "What?"

"You and I have to go back to your campsite and get that stash."

She gave an excited little gasp. "I'd like that. Seems kind of weird, but I miss my safe little cave."

And now, they would be driving directly into danger. Though Liam wasn't looking forward to what came next, he faced the windshield and nodded. "Let's get this over with."

"No problem." But Kate wasn't ready to move forward. Her mind was in the mountains. As soon as Liam had mentioned her campsite, she'd wanted to go back. With him.

Unfortunately, such solitude wouldn't be possible until they'd dealt with the immediate problems here in Denver. She cranked the key in the ignition and started the car. Using a back route and parking on a hillside, she showed him a secret path into the Carradine mansion, so they could avoid confrontation with the reporters who had settled along the circular drive at the front of the house.

"I used to come this way when I was a teenager," she said. "Sneaking in. Sneaking out."

"You were a troublemaker," he said. "Doesn't surprise me."

When they entered through the French doors to the dining room, the first person Kate saw was Jonathan Proctor. Usually, when she faced her ex-husband, there was a clenching of her stomach muscles and a tension behind her eyes—sharp little pangs of regret, faded anger and a sense of failure. But now, she felt nothing. Not even an emptiness. Jonathan had lost whatever claim he'd had on her emotions.

Utterly self-composed, she introduced him to Liam, and it pleased her to compare the two men. Liam was a few inches taller and much more manly. Jonathan was polished to a slick, high gloss.

"Jonathan," she said, "there are a few things we need to get straight. I was not abducted or held captive. For twenty-eight days, I survived very nicely in my own little campsite, where I built my own fires, hauled my own water and caught my own fish."

"Good for you." His monotone response was more appropriate for someone who'd just heard they were about to have a root canal. "I'm glad you're safely home. We're all glad."

"Not everyone," Liam said.

Jonathan glanced dismissively over his shoulder at him. "What does that mean?"

"Last night, a professional assassin entered Kate's house."

"I'm aware of that," Jonathan said. "It's what made me think of a possible abduction."

She watched as Liam strolled around the dining room table. His manner was casual, but she could tell that he was getting into position, much the way an attorney would maneuver in a courtroom.

"The assassin had a key," Liam said. "Other than the immediate family, who has keys for Kate's house?"

Forced to confront Liam head-on, Jonathan backed up a pace. "Someone who had taken her captive and stolen her purse."

"How would this captor know the code to disarm her alarm system?"

"Ask Kate." His smile was brittle. "Oh, but you can't. She has amnesia."

"She'll remember soon enough," Liam said.

She watched Jonathan's reaction. He was too professionally poised to betray his discomfort with anything obvious, like gulping or looking away. But she noticed a twitch in the fingers of his right hand, like a gunslinger waiting to draw.

Was he the person she ought to fear? Had Jonathan sent people to kill her? It was totally within his character to use hired assassins. And he had a motive for wanting her out of the way.

"While I was gone," she said, "you pushed through that project near Cougar Creek."

"I acted in the best interests of RMS. And for the environment. A lot of land in that area has been destroyed by fires."

"You knew I was opposed to development."

"Sorry, Kate. The project is already underway."

"I intend to stop it," she said.

"Now isn't the time to discuss business." His fingers twitched again. "You need to make a statement to the press."

Of course, that was also business—public relations to enhance the RMS image. The company was so much a part of her family that she'd given up trying to keep them separate.

Her mother swept into the room. "I thought I heard you in here."

"You were right, Mother."

Elizabeth gave her an air kiss on each cheek. "I have a lovely outfit for you, dear. And my stylist is here. We simply must do something with your hair."

Before Elizabeth could drag her off for a makeover, Kate latched onto Liam's hand. "Come with me."

She needed for him to be near her. He was the only person she trusted. He grounded her. The thought of being away from him—unprotected and vulnerable—was more than a little scary.

"My dear Kate," her mother said, "I'm sure Liam would be bored with all the primping."

"Not at all." He looked into Kate's eyes and responded to her desperation. Gallantly, he placed her hand on his arm as though he were escorting her to a grand ball. "Lead the way."

In her mother's upstairs bathroom, which was large enough to be a beauty salon, Kate was directed to a high stool in front of the mirror. While a stylist repaired the color in her hair and gave her a wispy cut, Kate kept an eye on Liam. Seated on a red velvet chaise in his denim work shirt, he looked big and rough-edged, incongruous as a moose among chipmunks. But he didn't seem uncomfortable.

Apparently, his masculinity wasn't threatened by a mob of women with lotions, potions and sprays. In fact, he seemed to be enjoying himself. An amused grin lifted the corners of his mouth as he allowed a manicurist to give him a hand massage and buff his fingernails.

Within an hour, Kate's hair was blown dry and her makeup applied. By conventional standards, she looked stylish and pretty. In the mirror, she met Liam's gaze. Though he nodded approval, she recognized a hint of regret in his expression, and she felt it, too.

All this grooming had suppressed Rain, the woman who had survived in the wilderness, the fighter, the self-sufficient survivor. Kate missed that independence—the challenge, and the satisfaction when she'd made it through another day.

"Fabulous," her mother said. "Slip into your new dress and you'll be ready to make your statement to the press. I'll be so glad when you do. I can't wait for those dreadful reporters to go away."

"What makes you think they'll leave?" Liam asked.

"They're waiting for Kate," Elizabeth said. "Once she's talked with them, they'll be satisfied. That's the way it works with a press conference."

"This is different," Kate gently corrected her. It was hard to believe that her mother, who was experienced at publicizing charity events, could be so naive. "This is a criminal case."

"Oh, please." Elizabeth glanced at her own reflection in the mirror and vaguely patted her hair. "You were lost and now you're found. There's nothing criminal about that."

"I'm talking about Wayne Silverman," Kate said. "He still hasn't—"

"I'm aware of the situation." Elizabeth's tone took on a sharp, imperious edge, befitting a woman of power and influence who could not be bothered with the details. "We have so many other things to worry about, darling. This weekend is the summer gala. You're aware of that, aren't you?"

"Yes, Mom. But—"

"As soon as you're done with your press conference, I need your help with the planning details."

In the mirror, Kate searched the reflection of her mother's eyes. Trying to discover what was really going on inside Elizabeth Carradine's head was like peering into a house where all the curtains were drawn. If the facts were cruel or brutal, Elizabeth dismissed them with a wave of her manicured hand. She always put up a good front. Her appearance was flawless. Her family was perfect and happy. And the show would go on. The summer gala would take place as scheduled. Never mind that someone was trying to kill her daughter.

"Mom? The investigating detectives are from Homicide."

Elizabeth stamped her foot. "This is not a criminal investigation until I say it is."

Was she covering something up? Protecting someone? "We have to face reality."

"Run along and get dressed, darling." Her smile was cold as the unmelted snow in the high Rockies. "All that's important right now is for you to make a good appearance."

With one final glance at Liam, Kate allowed herself to be led into the bedroom and dressed like a sacrificial lamb being prepared for the slaughter.

Chapter Eleven

While the head of the RMS public relations department directed the final choreography for her press conference, Kate waited inside the front foyer of her mother's house. The rest of her family—her mother, stepbrother, stepfather and ex-husband—had already trooped outside, and she was alone with Liam.

Nervously, she shifted back and forth on her high-heeled Gucci sandals. The outfit her mother had selected for her was a classic skirt and blouse of cream silk. Three-quarter sleeves covered the scar from the bullet wound on her upper arm.

She glanced over at Liam, who leaned against the wall beside the banister with his arms folded across his chest. He was solid as granite, utterly stable and self-controlled.

In contrast, a platoon of butterflies marched cadence in her stomach. "I don't want to do this."

"Come on, Kate. Everybody likes being a star, having their fifteen minutes of fame."

"Notoriety," she corrected. If she'd just won an Olympic gold medal or a WPGA tournament, she'd gladly welcome the attention. "The press is here to see for themselves if I'm cuckoo."

"You're not crazy," he said in a decisive voice that brooked no argument.

This was a man she could trust with her life; he would never lie to her. "How do I look?"

"Nice," he said.

She'd hoped for a bit more enthusiasm on his part. "Am I not gorgeous? Not sexy?"

"Your eyes," he said, "are beautiful."

When he stepped away from the banister and came toward her, she backed away. "No touching. You'll ruin my makeup."

He stopped in his tracks and hitched his thumbs in the pockets of his jeans. "Wouldn't want to mess up your lipstick. That would be a real tragedy."

An uncomfortable distance spread between them, and she didn't like the feeling. "My bag is packed, Liam. As soon as I'm done with this, I want to leave. We'll go back to the mountains. To my little cave."

"Are you sure?"

"Of course," she said. "I don't want to stay here."

"But you've got the big summer gala to plan. More clothes to buy. An image to protect."

"Stop it," she snapped. "I'm not my mother."

With his hands still stuck in his pockets, he leaned closer to her. "Why didn't you ask her about the necklace?"

"I couldn't. Not with all those people around."

As soon as she'd spoken, Kate knew she'd been mouthing a lame excuse. She didn't want to believe her mother was involved—even tangentially—in her disappearance. More than that, she feared that her mother might lie to her.

Through the front door, the PR director signaled to

Kate. She inhaled a deep breath and stepped through the front door to a makeshift podium. There she faced a couple dozen print, radio and television journalists. A cluster of microphones gathered at the edge of the lectern. Television lights glared. Cameras flashed.

Though she had spoken at press conferences and innumerable charity presentations, this was a different contingent of the media. Not the Society editor. Not the human-interest reporters who listened politely while she spoke about RMS contributions and the various projects they funded. These were crime reporters. Hardened and smart, this was the corps who'd provided the news on the Columbine massacre and the JonBenet Ramsey case. Politeness and tact weren't in their vocabulary.

She looked down at the one-page statement the public relations department had prepared for her. The words swam into focus and she read: "About a month ago, I got lost in the mountains, set up a campsite and survived using equipment that can be purchased at any RMS outlet."

She frowned at the blatant promotion from the public relations department. This was all wrong. She had these people here and needed to talk about something important.

Looking down at the statement, she continued. "I was found by a volunteer charter pilot working for CCC, Colorado Crime Consultants."

Another plug? She doubted that Adam Briggs wanted or needed publicity.

She concluded with a note her mother had written neatly in the margin. "I would like to take this opportunity to remind everyone of the annual RMS summer gala and silent auction, which will take place on Saturday night. Tickets may be purchased through RMS stores. Proceeds go to benefit several charities, notably, homeless shelters. Thank you for your interest."

Before she could turn away from the lectern and join her mother and family, who stood behind her, a trim, blond reporter called out, "Kate! Is Liam MacKenzie the pilot who found you?"

Though Liam had specifically asked that she not use his name, the press already had this information and there was no point in denial. Kate replied, "Yes."

That simple, one-word response opened a floodgate of other questions. Had she been injured? Did she have amnesia? Where was Wayne Silverman? Why were homicide investigators involved? What about the attack at her house last night? Was she being pursued by terrorists?

Slammed by this verbal assault, she looked over her shoulder, searching for Liam's reassuring presence. Instead, she saw her mother's frozen smile. Peter Rowe held Elizabeth's arm. His smile was rakish and charming. Not so with her stepbrother, Tom, who glared furiously, as if he'd like to declare open season on journalists.

It was Jonathan who stepped forward, supposedly to help her. His attitude was utterly condescending, as if he didn't think she could handle this crowd.

She'd show him! She returned to the microphone. These people wanted more than a brief statement; they had stories to file and news time to fill.

Kate held up her hand for quiet. She made eye contact, silencing their questions. Near the back of the crowd, she spotted Mickey Wheaton. He gave her a sign to call him, and she nodded. As far as she knew, Mickey had kept up his end of their bargain by not printing anything. She owed him.

When relative silence ensued, Kate said, "My family has always been concerned about environmental issues. My father, Eric Carradine, built RMS on his genuine love of the mountains and sports in general. I'd like to say a few words about how I survived for twenty-eight days in the wilderness."

For ten minutes, she talked about fire safety, foraging for plants, fishing and the natural bounty of the Colorado Rockies. She mentioned the basket she'd woven from twigs, and how she'd collected pebbles to keep track of the passage of time.

Though these journalists hadn't expected a lecture on the wilderness experience, they listened and took notes. It was a good story. In the back of her mind, she could see Mickey framing the headline—Kate Carradine: Survivor.

This was the aspect she wanted to focus on. Not her loss of memory. Not the grotesque reality of someone trying to kill her.

She concluded, "I hope to use my wilderness experience in establishing a mountain camp for disadvantaged kids, teaching them how to use the environment to survive."

As she turned to depart, a reporter called out, "If RMS is so big on environment, why the development at Cougar Creek?"

She glanced at Jonathan. It was almost too easy to take a potshot at his pet project, but she couldn't resist. "RMS's plans for that area will be reconsidered. In my opinion, the move toward development was undertaken with haste rather than due consideration."

With a quick pivot, she left the podium and returned to the house. Jonathan was right beside her. "What the hell have you done? I'm trying to raise investor capital for Cougar Creek."

"Think again."

"Things ran a hell of a lot better around here while you were gone."

That sounded like a threat. "Do you want me out of the way, Jonathan?"

"Don't push me, Kate."

They were interrupted by Elizabeth with her air kisses. "Thank you, darling, for mentioning the gala. This should give a boost to ticket sales."

If Elizabeth had heard a single word Kate had said about her struggle for survival, she gave no indication.

Peter sidled up beside Kate, gave her a one-armed hug and said, "Well done."

Her heart sank. If Peter approved, Kate knew she hadn't said the right things, the truthful facts that might include the murder of Wayne Silverman. "I didn't say enough."

"We can leave the rest to the public relations department and concentrate on getting you healthy."

"I'm not seeing a psychiatrist," she said.

"We only want what's best for you." He sounded smarmy, as usual. "We need to find out what's going on in that pretty little head of yours."

"Why? Why do you care what I might remember?"

"Amnesia and paranoid delusions?" He gave a genial and totally fake laugh. "Well, that can't be a good state of mind."

"Absolutely not," her mother echoed. "I believe it's time for tea, darling. Cook has prepared a snack."

Through the arch that led into the living room, Kate saw Detective Clauson talking to her stepbrother, who still looked angry. Though they weren't genetically related, Tom had his own version of the legendary Carradine temper.

The head of public relations and his assistant came toward her. The cook shoved a bottle of water at her.

Too many people! Too much pressure! Her head swam. Kate felt like a downed zebra in the midst of lions, all tearing away a piece of her.

Then she spotted Liam. He stood apart from the others. The calm reassurance in his hazel eyes was exactly what she needed. Liam was her safe haven in this maelstrom.

She caught hold of her mother's arm and whispered in her ear. "I need to get away from here. I'll only be gone a few days. Please don't worry."

"But where are you going?"

"Somewhere quiet." Though she wanted to be honest with her mother, Kate knew it wasn't wise to give out details. She couldn't talk about her plan to return to her former campsite.

"Maybe Aspen," her mother said. "It's lovely and cool this time of year."

"Lovely," Kate echoed as she escaped toward Liam.

Pausing only to grab the gym bag she'd packed and left on the staircase, and to change from her Gucci heels into sneakers, she led him through the house, through the kitchen and out the back door. Her intention was to run to where his car was parked. Then to the mountains. To her campsite.

In the gazebo at the edge of the property, Liam balked. "Wait."

Her feet itched with the urge to run away from here and find safety. "We have to hurry. I want to get away before the reporters figure out there's a back way into the property."

Instead of jogging along beside her, he took her hand and led her up the three steps to the center of the white, filigreed gazebo. Ironically, this very spot was where she'd stood before a pastor and recited her wedding vows. Another desperate mistake!

"You did okay with the press," he said.

She shook her head. "I didn't say enough. I should have mentioned Wayne Silverman. Should have talked about the assassin."

"It's not necessary to give the media all the details."

But telling the truth was important for her own emotional stability. She'd lived most of her life behind a facade. Now things had to be different. She needed to be more than an RMS shill, trying to sell more high-end sleeping bags.

She wanted to be a better person. For that to happen, they needed to figure out what had happened to Wayne Silverman. "We have to go. Now."

"We can't," he said.

"But we need to return to my campsite." Her voice held a note of desperation. "Right away."

"Clauson doesn't want you to leave town." As he watched, her face fell. The sparkle left her eyes. "I'm sorry, Kate. You're his only witness."

And his only suspect, Liam added to himself. While she'd been putting the finishing touches on her makeover, Detective Clauson had read him the riot act. When they'd fled her house and arrived at the motel, Liam should have reported in more frequently. No way should he have encouraged Kate to sneak out a window to escape a reporter. As a former assistant D.A., Liam should have known better.

"What about the things I hid?" she whispered. "We can't leave it unguarded."

"Nobody's going to find it. You were up there for a month, and nobody found you."

"It's evidence," she said.

"You're right," he said. "And we should tell Clauson about it."

"No." She looked up at him with alarm. "You didn't—"

"I wanted to," he said. It went against his grain to withhold information from an investigating detective. "But I promised you I wouldn't talk, and I've kept my word."

She set her gym bag down on the bench that circled the gazebo. When she turned to face him, her gaze was cool and sophisticated.

Liam hardly recognized this neat, attractive woman in silk. The makeover and the packaging put him off. In her designer outfit, she looked like everybody else—the attorneys he had worked with at the D.A.'s office, the wealthy folks who hired him for charter flights. Kate Carradine, in her chic hairdo and her untouchable makeup, wasn't the kind of woman he'd give a second glance. She was part of a world he had tried to leave behind when he'd moved to Grand Lake.

"I simply won't stay here at my mother's house," she said. "It's not safe."

"We'll go back to your place."

Her expression was disdainful. Kate was more like her mother than she cared to admit. "Are you referring to the house where we almost got killed?"

"I have a plan." He'd been on the phone and had made some arrangements. "Adam recruited a couple of bodyguards—retired military men who volunteer for CCC. They'll stand watch tonight."

Her eyes narrowed and her chin lifted. She didn't like being told what to do. He braced himself for another tantrum.

Instead, she only shrugged. "It seems I don't have a choice."

"Hey!" The shout came from the direction of the house. Tom stalked toward them. "What are you doing out here?"

"Getting grounded," Kate said. "In more ways than one."

"What's that mean?"

She shook her head. "I had to get away. There was too much going on inside the house."

"Tell me about it." He bounded up the stairs and joined them inside the gazebo. "This place is crazed."

Liam wasn't sure what to think of Kate's stepbrother. Though Tom was in his late twenties, he seemed younger, often behaving with the overblown petulance of a teenager. "Everybody's telling you what to do and what to say," Liam observed.

"No joke. My dad ordered me to stay away from the press and not to mention Wayne."

"Do you know him?"

"Sure." When Tom looked down to study the toes of his running shoes, his bangs fell forward and completely obscured his eyes. "Wayne was a good guy."

"Was?" The use of past tense might be significant.

Tom looked up. Hostility distorted his features. "You don't really think Wayne's still alive, do you? After a whole month?"

"What do you think?"

"Nobody gives a damn about what I think." His angry gaze slid toward Kate. Clearly, he resented the attention that came her way. "Anyway, I was supposed to come out here and get you. You're wanted back in the house."

She reached toward him, taking his hand in hers. Lightly, she stroked his cheek. "I'm sorry, Tom."

"Yeah, sure," he muttered.

"She's telling the truth," Liam said. "She cares about what happened to Wayne."

"But she still can't remember," he said bitterly.

Liam said, "I didn't realize you were so close to Wayne."

"We hung out," Tom said.

"We met someone else you might know. A reporter named Mickey Wheaton."

"Yeah, I know Mickey. Kind of a dork."

Someone else called to them from the house. Just as things were getting interesting with Tom, they were being drawn back into the Carradine family fold.

Quickly, Liam asked, "Did you ever hang out together? You and Wayne and Mickey?"

Tom pushed his long hair off his forehead and gave him a sneer. "I can't remember. Just like Katie."

Liar! It was obvious to Liam that Tom knew a hell of a lot more than he was saying. His secrets would put Kate in more danger.

Chapter Twelve

En route to her house, Kate and Liam drove in the Land Rover. In front of them was a patrol car with lights flashing but no siren. Then came Detective Clauson's unmarked car. Bringing up the rear was another police vehicle.

"It's a regular parade," Kate muttered. She'd resigned herself to the fact that she had to cooperate with the police and their insistence that she stay in town. But she was still unwilling to share all of her memories with Detective Clauson.

"So much for privacy," Liam said.

"Should we tell Clauson about the friendship between Wayne Silverman and my stepbrother?"

"And Mickey Wheaton," he reminded. "I'm sure the police have already questioned Tom."

She supposed he was right. And she knew for a fact that more than the Denver police department was involved. There were state crime investigators, mountain-rescue personnel and, of course, the sheriff near Grand Lake, who was looking into the vandalism at Liam's cabin. "I'd like to know the details of all these investigations. Do you think Clauson would tell us?"

"Doubtful." Liam shook his head. "Cops don't like it when amateurs like us get involved."

"Why not?"

"There's one big, fat, obvious reason," he said. "It's dangerous."

But she was already in danger. As they drove into her cul-de-sac, Kate's mind was racing. She had no intention of sitting idly by while the police followed up on leads. The truth was hers, locked in her memory. All she had to do was find the key.

At her front door, Detective Clauson himself removed the yellow crime-scene tape so she could enter, and she thanked him warmly. She wanted to have the detective on her side.

After Clauson deployed his men to search the house and set up a perimeter at the end of the driveway for the reporters who had followed, she invited him into the living room. Kate sat on the sofa with her feet tucked up under her. "Detective, I'm not sure if I've said this before, but I want to do everything possible to help you."

He remained standing, keeping his distance. "Have you remembered something that might help us locate Wayne Silverman?"

"I'm still thinking about his car." Carefully, she broached this difficult topic where her memories diverged from the factual evidence. "I was so certain that we had that car in the mountains."

"It's possible," Clauson conceded. "However, his Ford Explorer is now at his home."

"It might help me remember if I could go to his town house and see the car for myself."

Liam joined them. "That's true, Detective. Kate's

memory is stimulated when she comes in contact with physical objects."

The detective laced the fingers of his large hands together in an attitude that reminded her of prayer. He seemed wary as he considered her suggestion. "I need for you—both of you—to understand one thing. There will be no investigating on your own. If you have questions or suspicions, tell me."

"Of course," she said.

"I'll arrange for you to visit Wayne's town house." He went to the door. "Tomorrow morning."

"Thank you, Detective." She closed the door behind Clauson and turned to Liam. "Would you come upstairs with me for a moment?"

He followed her up to the bedroom, where he closed the door and leaned against it. "You're up to something."

"Solving the crime." She went behind the half-closed door of her walk-in closet to change clothes. "I certainly don't want to just sit here, locked up like a prisoner in my own house."

"Even if it's safe," he said.

Quickly, she slipped out of her cream silk outfit. From the gym bag she'd packed at her mother's house, she pulled out a pair of jeans and a collared jersey shirt. It was green—the color of money. "I won't be safe until this is over."

Though her new clothes were two sizes smaller than usual, they were still roomy. She frowned as she pulled out a handful of material at the hip. It was taking a while to become accustomed to this skinny body. A month ago, she'd been confident in her appearance, knowing that her curves were all in the right places—well-toned and shapely. Her formerly long hair had been an asset. And now?

She emerged from the closet. Her hands were on her head, wildly tousling the hairdo that had been created with such care by a stylist. "I hate mousse," she muttered.

"Big, mean animals," he said.

"And even worse in your hair."

She crossed her bedroom to the bathroom, where she washed off the heavy makeup that had been necessary for the glaring scrutiny of the camera. When she looked up into the mirror above the sink, she was disappointed. Had her chin always been that sharp? Her neck was like a pipe stem. Her thinner face seemed too sharply angled. Unfeminine. Scrawny. Plain.

Needing reassurance, she stepped out of the bathroom and faced Liam. "How do I look?"

Much to her surprise, his eyes warmed. "You're gorgeous."

"Wow." She was taken aback. "I didn't get a 'gorgeous' when I was all dolled up."

"I like you better this way. Natural."

"Are you sure?"

"The way I see it, there are two Kates. One is classy and well-dressed. A corporate woman."

She nodded. "You don't care much for her."

"She's like everybody else," he said with a shrug. "Proper and predictable. Always doing the right thing. Putting up a good front."

"And the other?" she asked.

"Outdoorsy. The other Kate enjoys sports. She wants to establish a mountain-survival camp. She's a little bit wild, untamed." His voice lowered to an intimate level. "A little bit sexy."

His compliments lifted her self-esteem by several notches. She could feel a blush rising in her cheeks, but she didn't quite believe him. Kate could see all sides of herself in the mirror. And none of them were particularly attractive.

Cautiously, she approached Liam. Unlike her, he had no reason for self-doubt. Any woman with eyes would rate him high on the macho scale. Any woman with breath in her body would be glad to have him hold her in his arms.

His smile invited her closer. Did she dare test his words? Kiss him? She reached up and placed her hand on his cheek. "You're being too kind."

"I'm telling the truth."

Though she trusted him implicitly when it came to friendship, she wasn't so sure about other areas. If she offered herself to him and he pulled away, she'd be crushed.

Quickly, she took a couple steps back. "Are you ready to see yet another side of me?"

"Let me guess," he said. "Nancy Drew, girl detective?"

"I'd choose a more grown-up role model. But, yes, I think we should be investigators."

"The police can handle this."

"I know more than they do," she said.

"Only because you haven't told them," he pointed out. "Kate, this isn't a game. Somebody wants you dead."

A glimmer of fear rose up inside her, but she suppressed it. "The only way to figure out what happened to Wayne is if I start remembering, and I don't trust that it'll come to me in a dream. I have to go after it, to chase the truth."

He exhaled a long-suffering sigh. "I've been around you too long. You're beginning to make sense to me."

"Then you agree?"

"I'll help you, but we take no risks. Is that clear?"

"Clear as the crystal goblets in my kitchen cabinets." She headed toward the bedroom door. "Which reminds me, isn't it time for dinner?"

She padded along the upstairs hallway toward the staircase. Though she'd outlined her goals and Liam had agreed, she didn't feel satisfied. There had been a missed opportunity in her bedroom. A promise of intimacy unfulfilled. She should have kissed him. Or maybe not. After all they'd been through together, she didn't want to do anything that might mess up their friendship.

Descending the stairs, she realized that, once again, she was operating from fear. In spite of all her stated bravado, she was scared that he didn't really want more from their relationship, that he didn't want her as a woman.

At the dining room table, beneath a chandelier made of intertwined antlers, Liam closed the lid on an empty pizza box. The melted mozzarella and pepperoni formed a pleasant lump in his belly. He took a sip of Coors.

"You know," Kate said as she licked a bit of pizza grease from her fingertip, "I'm a great cook. I should have made dinner."

"How? You've got nothing in your refrigerator."

"No problem. There's plenty to forage in the backyard."

"Oh, yeah, Nature Girl." Though he didn't doubt her cooking skills, the idea of edible xeriscape was definitely not a turn-on. Sarcastically, he said, "Too bad our body-guards told us to stay inside."

Liam was inclined to follow orders from these three CCC volunteers. All retired military, their hair might be gray, but their bearing was sharp as reveille in the morning. These three men were tough old birds. Two of them kept watch in her yard. Another, named Tony, wore a Navy SEAL patch on his leather bomber jacket. He patrolled inside the house.

"We ought to be safe," Kate said. "We've got the bodyguards. And there's a patrol car parked out front."

He nodded agreement. For once, imminent peril was not an issue.

"Plus," she said, "there are still three or four newspeople who appear to be spending the night. Speaking of reporters, I should return Mickey's phone calls. He's left a whole stack of messages on my cell—all of them are supposedly urgent."

Though Liam had a natural antipathy toward journalists, he had to admit that the weird little guy had provided some good information the last time he'd invaded Kate's property. "Do it. I want to ask him about his connection with your stepbrother."

While she made her call, Liam finished off his beer. Because they were well protected tonight, he intended to let his guard down and relax. Who knew what tomorrow would bring?

Kate disconnected her call. "Mickey says he has new evidence, and he'll be here right away."

Before Liam could react, there were sounds of a disturbance from the front of the house. A screeching voice identified himself as Mickey. Apparently, "right away" meant "right now"!

Liam and Kate hurried toward the front door and arrived simultaneously with Tony.

"It's okay," Kate said to him. "I called this guy. His name is Mickey Wheaton."

The former Navy SEAL shot Liam an unsmiling glare. "In the future," he said, "inform me of any arriving guests."

Outside the front door, they could hear Mickey's unintelligible yelling.

"Step back inside, ma'am," Tony said. His next order was for Liam. "When I open the door, disarm the security system."

"Right." If Kate hadn't been the victim of two prior attacks, he would have considered the bodyguard's attitude to be excessive. Under their current circumstances, he was grateful for Tony's vigilance.

When Tony opened the door, Liam caught a glimpse of Mickey Wheaton, cuffed and facedown on the sidewalk. Another CCC bodyguard loomed over him.

Tony hauled the little reporter inside. "Is this your guest?"

"You bet I am," Mickey snapped. With his hands still cuffed behind his back, his shoulders whipped back and forth. He looked like an angry bantam rooster.

"That's him," Liam said.

Quickly, Tony removed the cuffs. He offered no apologies as he stepped back into the shadows.

Mickey strutted toward the dining room, muttering about how he ought to sue. His feathers were ruffled. Grudgingly, he said to Kate, "Good job at the press conference. You didn't give away any of the good stuff."

"It was all good," she said. "Information about wilderness foraging and camping is useful."

"Yeah, yeah, yeah." He waved his hand, brushing away her comment. "The mountain-survival story is okay, but you know what people really want."

"What's that?" Liam asked.

"Sex and violence," Mickey said. "That's what sells."

"Sorry to disappoint," Kate said briskly. "On the phone, you mentioned new evidence."

"I'm tracking down a lead on Wayne Silverman, but I need your help. My source won't see me, but she'll talk to you, Kate."

"Who is this person?"

"Not so fast." He waggled a finger at her. "If I tell you, you could set up a meeting without me. I've got this arranged for tomorrow at one. At Shelby's Café."

"I know where it is," Liam said. "Not far from downtown Denver."

"At one," Mickey repeated. "Now, tell me about last night. Somebody came after you, right?"

"Whoa." Liam sat at the kitchen table. With his foot, he pushed out a chair for Mickey. "Sit. I've got a question for you."

Mickey lowered himself to the chair. He seemed even more high-strung than the last time they'd seen him. "What's up? What's the prob? What's happening?"

"Earlier today, we spoke with Kate's stepbrother. He mentioned that he knew both you and Wayne. That you hung out."

"Tom Rowe said that?" Mickey squeaked. He sounded like Mickey Mouse. "I don't know what he's talking about."

Liam knew a lie when he heard it. And this was a lie. "What's the connection with you three?"

"I guess, maybe, we all spend time in the same places. You know, the brewpubs in LoDo. But we're not pals. Me and them? Those guys are high-maintenance hot-shots, and I'm—"

"A future bestseller," Liam prompted. Mickey's

aspirations were high enough to match either Tom's or Wayne's. "A movie mogul."

"Not yet," he said. "And until I hit the big time, guys like Tom and Wayne aren't going to be buddies with a guy like me."

Liam still didn't believe him. "This is a dangerous situation, Mickey. If you know anything, you need to tell us."

"I don't." He turned to Kate, who had taken a seat beside him at the table. "About last night? Who came after you?"

"I probably shouldn't say anything."

"Give me a crumb," he pleaded. "Everybody else got stories. Give me something good. An exclusive."

She turned to Liam. "Should I tell him?"

There were a couple of details that shouldn't be divulged to the press. Like the fact that the assassin had a key and knew the code to disarm her alarm.

However, the police had a full report on last night's incident, and Liam knew it was only a matter of time before every tiny item was leaked to a more well-connected reporter, someone like pretty, blond Joyce and her ever-present cameraman. Liam took a perverse pleasure in the thought that the big news teams would be scooped by Mickey, the underdog. "Might as well give this man his exclusive."

She started talking, vividly describing the dark house and the experience of being stalked by a professional assassin. As she spoke, Liam sat back and watched the change of expression on her face. Her blue eyes darkened, then flashed wide. Her hands pantomimed holding the gun. Her slender shoulders hunched as if she were, at this very moment, hiding on the staircase.

A good storyteller, she caught and held Mickey's attention. He leaned forward, hanging on her every word. If Liam hadn't been there himself, he might have been drawn in, might have considered those intense moments of fear to be nothing more than a great adventure. But he knew better. He knew how terrified she'd been.

Her skill at hiding her true feelings amazed him. And it worried him, too. She was better than some pathological liars he'd come in contact with when he'd been a prosecutor. How much was she hiding from him? Was she capable of theft? Of murder?

His instincts told him no. Her ability to keep secrets was a survival technique—necessary in the complex world where she lived. In her family, she needed an iron-clad shell. But those defenses made it hard for him to understand who she really was and what she really wanted.

When she finished her story, Mickey was drooling for more.

Liam said, "Not until you tell us about this person we're meeting and their evidence."

"No way." Mickey shook his head. "You'll have to wait until tomorrow."

"We'll see you then." Abruptly, Liam took him by the shoulders and aimed him toward the door. Tony appeared and whisked Mickey back outside.

As soon as the reporter departed, Liam belatedly recalled something else he'd meant to ask about. He had wanted to check out Mickey's story about Peter Rowe making a copy of the diamond necklace.

"Give me your cell phone, Kate. I've got another question for Mickey."

He pressed Redial and was connected to Mickey's

cell phone. As soon as Liam identified himself, Mickey said, "Miss me already?"

"You told us about a jewelry store," Liam said. "Peter Rowe went there."

"That's right."

"What was the name of the jeweler?"

"I don't remember," Mickey said too quickly.

He was lying, again. No way would a reporter forget the details about such an important piece of information. "Where was it? The location of the shop?"

"I can't recall that, either. It's probably in my notes at home. I'll tell you tomorrow."

As Liam disconnected the call, he knew that Mickey Wheaton was playing his own game of secrets. Like Kate, he had something to hide.

Chapter Thirteen

Less than an hour later, Liam said good-night to Tony, the bodyguard, and followed Kate into her bedroom. It was after nine o'clock. Night had settled quietly in her cul-de-sac. Even the dog next door had stopped barking. There was no reason to feel apprehensive, but Liam's antennae were up. Something was going to happen tonight.

Kate grabbed a notepad and pen from the bedside table, then bounced to the middle of her bed, where she sat cross-legged. She was high on pizza and full of pep, revved on all cylinders. "This is the part where we make notes and cleverly solve the crime."

If only it were that simple. He settled into a white brocade chair beside her dresser, watching as she bent over the small notebook and energetically scribbled. With her head tilted downward and her elbows out at sharp angles, she was damn cute.

Thanks to her mother's stylist, Kate's wilderness hair had been tamed into calmer streaks of blond but was still tousled and wild. Her full lips parted slightly as she concentrated on the notepad in her hand. When the tip of her pink tongue ran across her lower lip, he was tempted to kiss her teasing little mouth, to pull her into his arms and...

Stop! He knew better than to play that dangerous game. Kate danced through life like a princess, taking what pleased her at one moment and discarding it the next. A kiss meant nothing to her.

She held up the notepad for him to see. "This is what we know."

He read. "A murder. The loot. Wayne missing."

The facts were as sketchy and vague as her memory. He suggested a different approach. "Let's talk about motive. Somebody is after you. Why? Who benefits from your death?"

"Nobody, really," she said. "When I die, all my stuff—property, trust fund, assets and shares of RMS—goes to my mom. With some bequests to charities."

"If the money goes to your mother," he said, "it ultimately passes to her husband and then to your stepbrother."

"Peter and Tom," she said. "Neither of whom need the money."

"Does Peter have an independent source of income?"

"I don't think so," she said. "He doesn't need one."

"Not unless he's thinking of leaving the Carradine family fold."

"Doubtful," she said. "I don't like Peter, but he's wonderful with my mom. And they had a prenuptial agreement that gives him a massive payoff in case of divorce."

When Liam had been an assistant D.A., the rule in any complex investigation was: follow the money. "RMS is a big, powerful company. With all these assets floating around, money has to figure into the motive."

"If I die, there would be a power shift on the board," she said. "I own a third of the company stock, which is enough to throw a wrench into developments I don't approve of."

"What about your mother? How much does she own?"

"Also a third. But Mom isn't interested in the business end of things. She generally goes along with the rest of the board."

"Including Jonathan."

"Right," she said.

He clarified. "She chooses Jonathan's opinion over yours?"

"My mother can be formidable when she wants to be. Most of the time, she doesn't bother with the business end of RMS. Jonathan makes money for the company. That's his job, and he's good at it." She sat up straighter. "He threatened me today. After the press conference, Jonathan told me that things went better at RMS when I wasn't around."

"So he has a motive for wanting you dead."

"It's kind of a stretch," she said.

He agreed. The idea that a CEO would arrange attacks by assassins to eliminate a problem on the board of directors was over the top.

Likewise, there was no obvious motive for Peter or his son. If they killed Kate, they would also have to kill her mother to benefit. "It's too complex. Too Byzantine."

"What are we left with?"

"The obvious motive—you witnessed the murder of Wayne Silverman. Wayne's killer needs to eliminate you before your memory kicks in."

"If it ever does." She gave a frustrated little bounce on the bed that turned his thoughts from their investigation toward the obvious fact that they were in her bedroom. The smooth fabric of her green T-shirt outlined her slender body. Her feet were bare.

"About Wayne," she said. "We don't have enough

information to know why anybody would kill him, but we can find out. Tomorrow, when we go to his town house with Detective Clauson, we'll look for answers."

With an effort, Liam dragged his thoughts back to their investigation. "When it comes to suspects, I keep returning to the big three—Peter Rowe, Tom Rowe and Jonathan Proctor." He shook his head. "I still don't get why you married that jerk."

"Blame it on my bad judgment in men."

Her answer was flip, too easy. "That's what was going on in your head. What about your heart?"

"Did I love Jonathan?" She sounded shocked by the concept. "I don't know. Sometimes, it feels like I've never been in love with anybody."

"Hard to believe." She was beautiful, vivacious and rich. "You must have had a hundred proposals."

"I'm talking about real love—perfect love, the kind that sweeps you off your feet. An all-consuming love is when the sight of your lover and the sound of his voice send thrills up and down your spine. And his touch? Oh my God, making love is pure pleasure. Every waking thought focuses on him. At night, he lives in your dreams."

As Liam listened, he fell under the spell of her story-making. Her perfect love sounded like a fairy tale. A pretty fantasy. "Go on."

"My perfect lover would make me laugh. Whenever anything happened, I wouldn't be able to wait to tell him. He would become my all—my past and present and, especially, my future. He's the person I want to grow old with."

"Is that how you felt about Jonathan?"

"Never." Her response was lightning quick. "I've

never felt that way about anyone. Maybe I settled for Jonathan because I never really thought true love would happen for somebody like me."

"Why not?"

"I'm competitive, aggressive. I take what I want, when I want it." She fidgeted on the bed. "Mom says I act more like a man than a woman."

His gaze slid over the angles and curves of her body. "No way would I mistake you for a man."

"That's very sweet."

She hopped off the bed and came toward the chair where he was sitting. Leaning down, she planted a light kiss on his forehead and pulled back.

Liam caught hold of her arm. Whether her teasing was intentional or not, he'd had enough of being treated like a useful appendage. If they were going to kiss, she damn well better mean it.

He rose from the chair. One arm encircled her slim torso, pressing her against the length of his body. His lips joined with hers. Hard and demanding, his tongue probed the silky interior of her mouth.

His grasp on her body tightened. Her breasts crushed against his chest. He could feel the flutter of her heart through her T-shirt. The clothing separating their bodies was a distraction. He wanted her naked.

Then, he ended the kiss and stepped back.

She stumbled back a pace and sat on the edge of her bed. "What happened?"

"I kissed you the way a man is supposed to kiss a woman."

"I don't understand."

"You came bouncing over here and gave me a peck on the forehead. Like I was your stepbrother."

"Just a friendly little—"

"Forget it." He was willing to put up with her little touches and her frequent insistence that he stay with her and protect her. But Liam would be damned if he allowed her to give him a kiss and a pat on the head as if he were a house pet. He warned her, "Don't start something with me unless you're willing to follow through."

"What if I am…willing?" she said.

He hadn't meant to throw down a challenge. Of course, he wanted to make love to her. But not like this. Not because she had to prove herself. Her blue eyes shimmered, and her lips trembled with such painful vulnerability that he backed off. "It's all right, Kate. Forget it."

Her hand raised, and she covered her mouth. Her voice was little more than a breath. "I want to make love."

She sounded like she was accepting a fate worse than death. Swell! He'd done a real fine job, driving through their relationship with all the sensitivity of a dump truck.

"I didn't mean to push you," he said. "You come across so strong that I forget what you've been through. Twenty-eight days in the wilderness. Assassins. Amnesia."

"But I—"

"Tell you what, Kate. This never happened. Drop it. Let's move on."

He shook his head and walked away from her to stand at her bedroom window. Pulling aside the drape, he peered at the patrol car parked at the end of the drive and the news van that staked out her cul-de-sac. Everybody was interested in Kate. Nothing about her was private.

Liam wanted to shove the window open and take a taste of fresh air. Or maybe to jump out and go splat on the sidewalk, saving himself the frustration of dealing with this woman who ran hot and cold. Kate Carradine, the socialite. The well-groomed mannequin. The competitor. Damn it!

He missed Rain.

"You don't understand," she said.

"Yeah, I'm an idiot." He bonked his head against the windowpane—not hard enough to hurt, but enough to remind himself to back off.

"Damn it, Liam. That's not what I meant."

Kate lowered her hand to her breast. Her heart was still beating fast. She'd gotten more from his kiss than she'd bargained for. Chimes had been ringing. An electric thrill had gone through her body, and she'd lost all control. Her knees were still weak.

She wanted to make love to him. To give herself. To take what he offered. This urge wasn't planned or programmed. Her need for him was as primal as survival.

When she pushed off the bed, her feet seemed to float above the hardwood floor—similar to the feeling after she'd ridden in his small plane. Walking on air. Her forward motion was a glide. She was impelled toward him like the tide pulled by the gravitational force of the moon.

Before she entered his universe, she hesitated. Her gaze swept from his thick, brown hair to his boots, pausing on the way to notice broad shoulders and a fine butt. A good-looking man, for sure. But he was so much more. He was honest and smart and he made her laugh. He was someone she might fall in love with. True love. With all the frills.

With Liam, she might find the kind of all-consuming relationship she'd never thought possible. But did she dare take that risk?

Her heart beat even faster. She wanted him. No matter what the emotional risk.

In two quick strides, she was beside him. "I never meant to be a tease."

"Forget it."

Slowly and purposefully, she turned him away from the window and wrapped her arms around his neck. In a clear voice, she said, "Make love to me."

He took her arms and firmly lowered them. His gaze maintained steady contact with hers. "No."

She shuddered. It felt as though a bucket of ice water had been dumped over her head. "You don't think I'm attractive."

"Hell, yes. From the first time I saw you, I liked the way you looked. Wild and passionate. You're amazing."

"Then why—"

She had no more patience for words. Frantically, she wrenched free from his grasp. She threw herself at him.

Her kiss held nothing back. She pressed hard against his mouth. Her tongue probed. Her passion was true. She couldn't deny it for one more second.

He held back, unmoving and stiff. By his actions, he rejected her. With a gasp, she jerked her head away from his.

"I won't give up," she said. "Not until—"

"Shut up, Kate."

His arms closed around her, and his mouth claimed hers with a tenderness that brought her to the edge of tears.

His caresses were firm and strong, but gentle at the same time. His touch possessed the soft flesh of her breasts. His lips fed her desire for more.

She had demands of her own. Her fingers clawed at the buttons on his shirt, and she flung aside the material, baring his muscular chest and torso. Greedily, she stroked the fine, black hair on his chest. The tips of her fingers vibrated with hot, intense desire.

Their lovemaking grew—unchoreographed and wild as they tore away their clothing. Her gasps of surprised arousal mingled with his growls of pleasure.

Together, they fell onto her bed. Their legs twined together. She clutched at his body, wanting more and more. Everything! All that he could give.

His response was more than she'd even hoped for. First, he was on top. Then, she rolled over to take his place.

Intense and primitive, her need for him was as desperate as her need for survival.

He flipped her again to her back and loomed over her. His hazel eyes shone with a dark flame. His chest heaved. "Condom," he said.

"Drawer." She frantically pointed to her bedside table.

He lifted himself off her. Tearing through the contents of her drawer, he threw aside a book she'd been reading, a notepad, a pencil. Ripping open the condom package, he sheathed himself.

He straddled her. His body was magnificent, powerful, strong. Never had she seen a more perfect man. She yanked him down on top of herself, welcoming the pressure of his weight on her body.

They rolled again across the bed. Again, he was above her. Her thighs parted, and he entered her with a hard thrust. She closed around him, tight and moist. More, she wanted more. Bucking furiously, wantonly, she cried out as waves of pleasure spasmed through her body. Her flesh was sensitized from her toenails to her scalp. Nothing had ever been like this. No pleasure had ever been so intense. She climaxed as he did.

Gasping, he fell beside her on the bed. "You're amazing," he said. "Rain, you are amazing."

She lay back on the pillows, trembling and content. He had called her Rain. And she was glad. In her life as Kate Carradine, she had never been capable of such perfect, primitive lovemaking.

Chapter Fourteen

The next morning, Kate dressed casually but carefully in designer jeans, with a coral linen camp shirt, sandals and jewelry—including diamond stud earrings. She wanted to look as pretty as she felt after last night. Their love-making hadn't been the sweet, pink-icing fantasy of fairy tales. It had been wild and primitive and much, much better.

Riding in the backseat of Detective Clauson's sedan, she reached over to take Liam's hand. The mere act of touching him caused her heart to flutter. Looking at him made the insides of her eyeballs steamy and hot.

Holding his palm between her thumb and forefinger, she pinched with her nails. And when he glanced at her, she ran her tongue across her lower lip. In her classic blouse and diamond studs, she might look like the Kate Carradine who was a major stockholder in RMS. But when they were alone, she wanted him to know that she was Rain—earthy as the untamed forests of the Rocky Mountains.

The smoldering heat in his eyes echoed her passion. Oh, yeah, he wanted her.

Over his shoulder, Clauson said, "I'm not sure what

you two expect to find at Wayne Silverman's place. Forensics has been over everything. They found no sign of blood. No forced entry. No struggle."

"Fingerprints?" Liam asked.

"Sure, we found plenty of prints. A lot of them unidentified."

"How can that be?" Kate asked.

Liam explained, "Not everybody's fingerprints are included in the police data banks. Think of all the people who might come in and out of a house. Guests. Service people. Solicitors. They leave behind prints that could stay there for months."

Kate asked, "What about Wayne's car? Did you do forensics on the car?"

"Parked in the garage," Clauson said. "It's nice and real clean. Nothing unusual about it."

Wayne's two-story town house in central Denver wasn't marked with yellow crime-scene tape. As far as the police knew, nothing criminal had happened here. The two-story tan-brick structure looked innocent enough, with well-tended landscaping that matched the other three adjoining town houses. The window blinds were drawn as if hiding a secret.

As she strolled up the concrete sidewalk, Kate knew she'd been here before. The details were more eerie than déjà vu. She remembered the stone urn filled with red and white petunias. She had been here with Wayne. Had they been talking about their camping trip? Discussing where they should go? Their conversation faded unintelligibly in her mind, as people talking behind a glass wall.

Inside the town house, she noted the staircase. She'd never been upstairs. To the right was a home office, cluttered.

Clauson entered the office first. "So, Kate, does this bring back any memories?"

"I've been in this room before."

She squinted, trying to bring her memories to the surface. Her gaze surveyed the file cabinets, the surface of the desk that was covered with stacks of papers, unopened mail, a lamp, a telephone, stapler, tray of paper clips. Cardboard file boxes scattered across the light gray carpet.

Liam sauntered over to the desk and picked up an envelope. "This doesn't look like the desk of someone who was planning to leave town forever."

"That's what I thought," Clauson said. "There's a lot of unfinished business here."

"Did you check Silverman's financial information?"

"You bet."

Liam asked, "Anything odd?"

"Silverman stopped paying his bills after he took off for the camping weekend."

"When he disappeared," Liam said. "No use of credit cards? No activity in a checking account?"

"Nothing," Clauson said. "Two days before he went missing, Silverman opened an offshore bank account in the Caymans. We had to pull a lot of strings to get a court order to open it." He nodded to Kate. "Your mother's influence helped."

"And what did you find?"

"After the initial thousand bucks, there were no deposits or withdrawals."

Though Kate wasn't an expert on offshore banking, she knew those accounts were a potential way to hide large deposits—like the cash she'd found in the backpack. Someone like Wayne Silverman, who knew the legal ins and outs of handling money, would be expert in manipulating such an account. He must have opened it in anticipation of making a large, untraceable deposit.

But the cash in the pack was fifty thousand—not an unconscionably huge amount. A quick glance at the possessions carelessly arrayed in this town house told her that his tastes were expensive. He wouldn't give this up for less than a million bucks.

Liam held up a framed photograph of a bunch of guys in baggy jerseys and jeans. "This looks like a beer-league baseball team."

"The RMS team," Kate said. "Jonathan is the coach and star pitcher."

She moved closer, to study the photograph, and pointed to a shaggy-haired young man on the end. "There's Tom."

"Your stepbrother," Clauson said. "He and Wayne were friends. Matter of fact, Tom took Wayne Silverman's disappearance hard."

Her stepbrother's name kept coming up in association with Wayne Silverman, and she couldn't help wondering if their friendship had sinister overtones. What if they'd plotted the theft of the jewelry together and then had a falling out? Tom had a bad temper, and he was an expert marksman. But was he capable of murder?

She followed Detective Clauson and Liam through the kitchen, which was also messy. A couple of dishes in the sink were caked with dried food. The tile floor was grungy. They entered the garage, where Clauson turned on the light.

The black Ford Explorer was spotless and shiny. "This isn't right," she said.

"What do you mean?" Clauson asked.

She opened the driver's-side door and peered inside. "You saw the house. Wayne was never this tidy. The side pockets of the Explorer were stuffed with credit-card receipts. On the floor in the backseat, there were crumpled-up bags from fast-food joints."

She climbed up into the seat. "The dashboard was dusty."

"Maybe he stopped at a car wash," Clauson said.

Reaching across the seat, she opened the glove compartment. Inside was nothing but an owner's manual.

"This isn't right," she repeated, as she leaned back in the seat and stared through the windshield at the un-painted wood wall of the garage. Her vision blurred, and she closed her eyes.

Memory of her own voice resounded loudly in her head.

"Where are we going? My God, how do we get away from here?"

In the passenger seat beside her, she saw the slouched figure of a man. Wayne. It was Wayne. His chest was covered with blood. His fingers clutched at the wound, but he couldn't stop the bleeding. She had to get him to a doctor.

He groaned as the Explorer jolted along a narrow one-lane dirt road bordered by tall conifers on either side. Branches whipped against the car, battering the doors and windows of the car. She was driving fast, driving blind, unable to see more than twenty feet in front of her.

Dizzy from fear, she wrenched the steering wheel to stay on the path. Pain exploded in her arm where she'd been shot.

The Explorer crested a hill. Fire! She stared in terror

at the line of the blaze. No one but a crazy person would continue. But she had to go this way. It was the only escape.

The road ended. They could go no farther. "Wayne, we're going to have to go on foot."

"Tom," he whispered. "Tom, that bastard. He knows."

She opened her eyes and blinked. What had Wayne meant? *Tom knows.* Was her stepbrother the person who'd been pursuing them? Wayne had cursed him with what seemed like his dying breath.

She needed to tell the police. Tom knows! Her memory was vivid. But did she dare trust her own shaky memory? They had just seen the photo of Wayne and Tom. Her stepbrother was on her mind. Kate couldn't be sure that she hadn't made this up—tailoring her recall to reflect her suspicions.

Detective Clauson touched her arm, startling her. Quickly, she said, "I know I was in this car. Wayne was in the passenger seat. He was injured. We were driving toward a forest fire."

When she looked at Clauson, she saw disbelief in his eyes. "This vehicle," he said, "is clean. It wasn't anywhere near a fire."

She couldn't be wrong about this. Twice, she'd had a similar memory. The picture was so vivid, so impossibly accurate. She could see the low-hanging branches on the trees, could smell the smoke.

Her fingers rubbed the beige leather of the seats. "There should be bloodstains."

"We checked," Clauson said. "There were no blood spatters."

Liam asked, "What did they find in the way of fingerprints?"

"Nothing much." Clauson shrugged. "What are you getting at?"

"A hunch," Liam said. "Would you mind checking to find out about the prints?"

The detective pulled out his cell phone. "I can do that."

As Detective Clauson exited up the stairs into the house, Liam came to stand beside her. Lightly, he caressed her arm. "What did you remember?"

"It was the same as before." Tremors raced up and down her spine. The terror of her escape flowed in her blood. "Only with more detail. There was a lot of blood. And I thought I heard Wayne mention my stepbrother. Tom knows."

"What does he know?"

"I can't say. It wasn't clear. Maybe I'm just thinking about Tom because of the photo in Wayne's office. I'm not sure." Hopelessly, she gestured to the car seats. Even if they'd been cleaned in a car wash, there ought to be bloodstains in the stitching. "Maybe I'm losing my mind."

"You're fine," he said.

His eyes reassured her. She slipped off the car seat and into his arms. Her cheek nestled against his soft cotton shirt, and she absorbed the warmth and security of Liam's embrace.

A ragged breath escaped her lips. "You believe me, don't you?"

"Yes." He dropped a light kiss on her forehead. "When you were in the car, do you remember where you were?"

"There was a forest fire. Directly in front of the car. I was going toward it."

"We can check this out," he said. "I'll contact Molly at CCC, and she can pull up a map of where forest fires were burning on that day."

It had been a bad summer for fires in Colorado. "That might encompass quite an area."

"Not when we combine it with where you ended up."

"Are you sure? It seemed like I walked for miles and miles."

His smile warmed her. "Trust me on this. I do aerial photography. I'm good with maps."

Clauson returned to the garage. His heavy brow pulled down in a scowl. "Here's the story on fingerprints from the vehicle," he said gruffly. "Three different sets of unidentified prints."

"And none of them belonged to Wayne Silverman," Liam said.

"Correct."

"I thought that might be the case."

Kate glanced up at him. "I'm not sure what this means."

"Maybe nothing," Liam said. "But if Wayne Silverman returned this car to his garage, his prints should have been on the wheel."

"What if he was wearing gloves?"

"It's summer. Not the season for gloves." Liam continued. "The fact that there are none of his prints in his own vehicle makes me think the interior of this car has either been scrubbed down or replaced." He ran his finger along the pristine fender. "Maybe even a new paint job."

"It's possible," Clauson said. "I'll put some men out on the street to check with paint and interior detailing shops. Damn it. We should have noticed this."

Liam was more forgiving. He'd been on the investigating end—hard, thankless work. It was impossible to think of everything. "Why would you worry about the car? It looked okay. And you don't have a body. This is a missing-person case."

"A very high-profile missing person." Clauson turned to Kate. "Is there anything else? Any other memories?"

When she shook her head, Liam gritted his teeth. He wished she'd tell Clauson about Tom. If her stepbrother knew something, the police could put pressure on him. Maybe they'd get the truth.

At the same time, Liam recognized her fear—a level of panic that left her mind paralyzed and unreliable. She wasn't sure what was truth and what was…something else.

In the meantime, the police had a solid clue to investigate with the Ford Explorer. If they were lucky, the shop that had worked on Silverman's car would have details about who'd brought it in. And who'd paid for the repair work.

"Detective," he said, "there's another lead—involving Kate's memory—that I want to track. The forest fires."

Though Clauson scowled, he also nodded. "How?"

"Comparing maps of forest fires with the location where I found her. With aerial photos of the area, Kate might recognize the terrain."

Clauson's reluctance to use them in his investigation was apparent. "Where would you get these maps?"

"We can use the resources at CCC." Though Liam was sympathetic to Clauson, he didn't want to farm this work out to the police. "I'm an expert. I do aerial photography."

The detective aimed a finger at Liam. "And you'll tell me exactly what you find."

"Yes, sir."

"Do it," Clauson said. "I'll arrange for a ride to CCC."

Finally, it seemed that they were making progress toward a solution. A good sign. Liam smiled to himself. Everything would be all right. Everything would be rosy. It had to be. Since last night, when he'd made love to Kate, his whole world was painted with an optimistic glow.

THE FIRST TIME KATE HAD been at the Colorado Crime Consultants offices in Golden, she and Liam had just fled from the vandals who'd attacked his cabin. She'd newly departed from her mountain sanctuary, and her brain had been overwhelmed—numbed by the glare of commerce and deafened by the roar of traffic and conversation.

Now that she was more acclimated to civilization, she could appreciate this charming Victorian house that had been converted to office space. Inside was a foyer with hardwood floors, an imitation Persian rug and several potted ferns. Colorado Crime Consultants was the first door to the right.

Behind the antique front desk sat Molly Griffith. Her long, blond hair swooped across her forehead, and she wore more makeup than was typical for a secretary, including turquoise eyeshadow that matched her form-fitting, gauzy blouse with tasseled sleeves. She sashayed out from behind the desk and greeted them with the genuine warmth Kate remembered.

"Hungry?" Molly asked.

"Starved," Kate said. They hadn't had time for breakfast.

Molly cast a chiding look at Liam. "You've got to feed this woman. Kate probably had better access to nutrition while she was stranded in the mountains."

Reaching into her desk, Molly pulled out a gold-foil box and opened the lid. "It's Godiva truffles. One of our volunteers, Dr. Blair Weston, sends a box every month. She's a medical examiner, totally brilliant and also a choco-holic."

Liam said, "So's Kate."

"Am not," she responded.

"The only way I could lure you out of your cave was by waving a candy bar."

Though it had only been a few days, their first meeting seemed like years ago. Hadn't she known Liam forever?

She picked out a dark-chocolate truffle and immediately bit into it. Creamy and rich, the chocolate melted on her tongue. "Delicious."

"Take another," Molly said. "And you, Liam. Have some chocolate."

Adam Briggs came out of his office. "They didn't come here to eat."

"You will notice," Molly said dryly, "that I'm not offering you a piece."

As Kate savored her chocolate, she watched the snappy interaction between Molly and Briggs, as he informed her of the deleterious effect of sugar and she countered with the emotional benefit of eating chocolate. CCC was founded eight years ago, which meant that Molly and Briggs had been together longer than a lot of married couples. Kate wondered if they had ever been more intimate than office manager and director. Probably not. Briggs was far too straitlaced.

He folded his arms across his chest and pulled in his chin. "Molly, do you have the maps Liam wanted?"

"In the conference room."

With Molly in the lead, they entered a long room with a solid-oak table and a single large window at one end. Above the wainscoting, the walls were painted a deep red. Several framed maps hung across one wall. Molly pointed to one with a fingernail that was nearly as red as the wall color. "I think this is your work, Liam."

"I remember," he said. "This is the area where we located…a body."

"A reminder," Briggs said. "You're lucky, Kate. Most missing-persons cases don't have a happy ending."

"I am lucky." Her gaze drifted toward Liam. Meeting him might be the luckiest thing that had ever happened to her.

"Should I order lunch?" Molly asked.

"Not necessary," Liam informed her. "We have an appointment for lunch at one. Briggs said he'd take us there."

Briggs checked his watch. "We'll leave at twelve hundred, to make sure we're on time."

"Twelve hundred?" Kate questioned.

"A military thing," Molly said. "He means noon."

"Half an hour from now," Liam said. That was the time they'd arranged to meet with Mickey and his mysterious source—a meeting that Liam didn't feel entirely comfortable about.

He would have preferred having Clauson in the picture, but there was no chance of that. Mickey, the reporter, would undoubtedly go to extreme lengths to keep his source confidential.

Liam frowned. Another secret. There were altogether too many hidden agendas in this investigation. Kate's secrets. Mickey's source. And now, Tom. What did Tom know?

Approaching the stack of maps on the conference-room table, Liam started shuffling through them. Not only had Molly accessed the standard GPS-satellite maps, but there were also forest-service maps and a surveyor's chart. "Excellent job, Molly."

"The red Xs indicate areas where there were forest fires one month ago," she said.

It pained him to see so many red marks. Though many of Colorado's forest fires were due to natural causes, the destruction of old-growth forests was hard to accept. Towering pines and abundant plant life were reduced to charred stubs. The earth was scorched, wildlife scattered.

"If you'll excuse us," Molly said. "I need to clear the schedule for a couple of hours. Briggs, come with me."

Muttering about never having a minute to himself, he trailed her out of the conference room.

"They're cute together," Kate said.

"Don't ever let Briggs hear you calling him cute."

"They bicker like an old married couple, but you can tell they're fond of each other." She cocked her head to one side. "Do you think we'll ever be like that?"

It was hard to imagine that far into the future. Their relationship could be counted in hours instead of years. "I can't see that far ahead. The flame from last night is still too bright. And hot."

"Hot like this?" She slipped her arm around his neck and pressed against him. Her lips met his, passionate and hungry.

A fire started in the pit of his belly. Molten heat spread through his veins as he kissed her back. He should be wary, should remember the devastation of a raging wildfire. But her kisses felt too good. He loved the burn.

Slowly, he drew away from her. The taste of Kate and chocolate lingered on his mouth. He couldn't tear his gaze away from her beautiful face, her enchanting blue eyes.

Hearing Molly clear her throat, he turned toward the

door to the conference room in time to see the tall blonde stalk inside. Her attitude of fake indifference told him that she'd already seen their embrace.

"How are the maps?" she asked.

"I'll need to take them with me."

"Not a problem. These are duplicates."

Kate backed away from him. Her cheeks flushed red, a result of either sudden passion or embarrassment. Liam couldn't guess which, but he hoped it was the former.

She pulled out her cell phone. "I should call Mickey to confirm our appointment."

Liam nodded, watching the casual sway of her slender hips as she left the conference room to make her call.

He and Molly gathered up the maps and filed them in an oversize, padded envelope to accommodate the varying sizes and widths.

Molly carefully folded the forest-service map and handed it to him. "You and Kate," she said. "You look good together."

"That's funny." Liam cocked an eyebrow. "We were just saying the same thing about you and Briggs."

"That old curmudgeon? No way." Molly tossed her hair. "I may be past thirty, but I'm not that desperate for a man."

Glaring at her cell phone, Kate returned to the room. "I couldn't reach Mickey. But I answered a call from my mom. She has an emergency."

"A real emergency?" Liam questioned.

"To her, it is. Ticket sales for the summer gala on Saturday are booming, and there's a problem with the caterer. I need to stop by Mom's house."

As far as Liam could see, the caterer wasn't Kate's problem. "Your mother can handle this."

"She's overwhelmed," Kate said. "I've taken care of these arrangements for years."

"I understand," Molly said. "I have a friend who's a wedding planner. These big events are incredibly complicated. Why don't I come with? I'm pretty good at organizing."

From what Liam had seen, Molly was nearly a genius when it came to balancing the complex affairs of CCC. Kate's mother would be lucky to have her assistance.

Briggs appeared in the doorway. "Time to go."

Chapter Fifteen

Briggs dictated the seating arrangements for the drive into town—men in the front, women in the back.

As they headed away from the CCC offices in Golden, Liam found it difficult to be separated from Kate. He had an irrational urge to stay in physical contact, close enough to touch her silky hair and smell the wisp of perfume she'd applied this morning. The fragrance was a delicate mixture of orange blossom and musk that seemed natural, though it probably cost a small fortune.

Gradually, Liam realized, he was becoming more and more accustomed to Kate's classy looks, her jewelry, her sophistication and her wealth. Those things were part of the total package. The RMS heiress came along with Rain. Which really wasn't such a bad thing. How could he complain that she was too rich? Too well-connected? Too pretty?

He forced himself to tear his gaze away from her and looked at Briggs. "The bodyguards you sent to Kate's house last night did an excellent job."

Briggs gave a quick nod. "Good men. They like the opportunity to stretch their muscles now and again."

"I have a feeling they stay in damn good shape."

"Use it or lose it," Briggs said. "At this café, is there any reason to suspect danger?"

Though Liam doubted that a hit man would strike in the middle of downtown Denver, he said, "We can't be too cautious."

"My thought exactly." Briggs lifted his lapel to show the shoulder holster under his blazer. When it came to exercising the bodyguard muscles, Adam Briggs was no slouch himself. "Tell me the purpose of this meeting."

"Mickey Wheaton is a reporter who's done a lot of research on Kate. He claims to have a source with evidence."

"Evidence of what?"

"The reason Kate and Wayne Silverman disappeared in the mountains."

"Which is?"

"I don't know," Liam said.

"If you uncover any clues," Briggs said, "you'll be turning them over to Detective Clauson. Right?"

Liam nodded. He knew the police were better equipped to follow up on investigation. His only real goal was to keep Kate safe.

Outside Shelby's Café in the Governor's Park area of Denver, where many of the beautiful, old mansions had been preserved as office space or condos, Briggs parked illegally in a loading zone. "Molly and I will stay with the car," he said. "Liam, are you armed?"

He shook his head. It was warm today, and he wore only jeans and a white cotton shirt with the sleeves rolled up. There hadn't been a place to hide the Glock.

"Glove compartment," Briggs said.

Liam reached inside. There was a .22-caliber automatic pistol in an ankle holster.

"You're not licensed to carry this weapon," Briggs said. "But I don't want you to walk into a possible trap unarmed."

From the back seat, Kate piped up. "I'm sure Mickey would never do anything to hurt me. He thinks I'm his meal ticket."

"The reporter doesn't worry me," Briggs said darkly. "But you've already been attacked once by a professional. Remember that, Kate. Keep your guard up."

Liam remembered all too well. She was in danger. Everywhere she went. Every move she made. Danger.

Though the ankle holster felt clumsy, he was glad to have the firepower. He glanced through the passenger window toward the restaurant, where sidewalk tables were filled with patrons on this sunny Colorado day. "I don't see Mickey."

"A bad sign," Briggs said. "If he set you up, he might not want to be present for the attack."

Oh, yes, he would. Liam couldn't imagine Mickey passing up a scoop. Another attack on Kate? He'd be here with eighteen cameras hanging around his scrawny neck.

Kate pointed. "That's Rachel Robertson."

"Where?"

"The redhead with turquoise jewelry."

A tall woman stood in the shadow of the awning. Tucked under one arm was a large folder.

"You've mentioned her before," Liam said. "Who is she?"

"Rachel oversees three different shelters in the downtown area. The woman is a saint, completely dedicated to her work with the homeless. RMS has been funding her for years."

Rachel impatiently checked her wristwatch. She appeared to be waiting for someone. Liam wondered aloud, "Could she be Mickey's source?"

Briggs said, "There's only one way to find out. Approach her."

Leaving the car with Kate at his side, Liam scanned the outdoor tables. It was a casual, urban crowd. No one stood out. No one sat at a table alone. His gaze darted toward the shop on one side of Shelby's Café. A health food store. Could there be an assassin lurking among the herbal tea and homeopathic remedies?

As they came closer to Rachel, the red-haired woman gave them a warm smile and came forward to hug Kate.

"I was worried about you," Rachel said.

"You know me," Kate said. "I may take a tumble, but I always land on my feet."

"After all these years planning fund-raisers, I should have known that." Rachel cocked her head to one side as she studied Kate. "You look different."

"Well, I lost a lot of weight. And the hair—"

"It's something else. I've never seen your eyes so bright. It looks like you swallowed a jar of lightning bugs. You're…happy."

"I've been happy before," Kate said.

"Not like this."

Liam immediately liked this natural-looking woman with her tan made up entirely of freckles. Heavy turquoise-and-silver bracelets circled her bare, well-toned arms. Her smile and handshake showed a firm, unflappable strength. "Were we supposed to meet you?" he asked.

"Mickey said to come here. But I don't see him anywhere around." She shrugged and placed her folder in Kate's hands. "Here's the information he requested."

"What is it?"

"Accounting records," she said. "Of course, I refused to hand over this confidential data to a reporter."

"Of course," Kate said. As she glanced to the left, she saw three people at an outdoor table eyeing her curiously. Her photograph was all over the newspapers and television. It was only a matter of time before somebody recognized her.

Though she was accustomed to being noticed, this scrutiny was different. She felt freakish. "I'm afraid if we stay for lunch, the reporters are going to descend."

"I understand," Rachel said. "You're the flavor of the week, and everybody wants a taste."

"Do you have any idea why Mickey wanted this information?"

"He just said that you needed it." She clasped Kate's hand. "If there's anything else I can do to help, let me know."

As she met Rachel's calm, blue eyes, Kate saw an honest concern. With everything else this woman had to worry about—finding shelter, food and medicine for disenfranchised citizens—it seemed impossible that she could squeeze out another drop of compassion.

"Someday soon," Kate said, "you and I are going to establish that camp for kids. I learned so much while I was in the mountains."

"In the meantime, I'll see you on Saturday at the summer gala." Rachel hugged her again. "I love that you plugged the event at your press conference. You're a good person, Kate. Never forget that."

If she was such a stalwart, upstanding member of the community, why was someone trying to kill her?

AT THE CARRADINE MANSION, Briggs maneuvered his car through a veritable parking lot of news vehicles. Liam counted five broadcast vans from television outlets. Apparently, Kate's return had become national news. Mickey ought to be thrilled. And where was that little weasel? The fact that he hadn't showed for their appointment was worrisome.

Briggs got as close to the front door as possible, and Kate made a mad dash inside. Though the police kept the reporters at bay, there was a lot of shouting for attention. Long-range lenses aimed over the shrubs. Liam wondered if anyone was patrolling the rear entrance to the property, where he and Kate had parked the day before. "You'd think they had something better to take pictures of."

"I'm not anxious to step out there," Briggs said.

"Don't worry," Molly said as she exited the car. "I'll distract them."

She climbed out of the car on the side facing the reporters. Tossing her hair, Molly posed and waved like a prom queen.

Briggs turned to him. "I wanted a private word with you, Liam. Without Kate being around."

"Shoot."

"Are you withholding information from the police?"

Liam met his gaze. He couldn't lie to Briggs. "I haven't told Clauson everything. I promised Kate that I wouldn't."

"You know better," Briggs said. "You used to work for the D.A.'s office."

But he wouldn't betray her. No matter what.

Briggs continued. "This is a missing-person investigation. A probable homicide. You need to come clean with Detective Clauson."

"I need to respect Kate's wishes," Liam said. "She comes first."

"Does she feel the same about you?"

"I don't know." Liam wanted to believe she did.

Briggs's steely eyes narrowed. "Kate is the kind of woman who always gets what she wants. Be careful she's not playing you."

Molly tapped on Briggs's window. "Are you guys coming, or what?"

Briggs retorted, "Are you done acting like a starlet at the Cannes Film Festival?"

"They've got telephoto lenses," she said. "I might as well give them something to shoot."

Under his breath, Briggs muttered, "If she wasn't so good at her job, I'd fire her ass."

"That would be a damn shame," Liam said. "Molly has a fine ass."

He grabbed the oversize envelope, containing maps, and the financial folder from Rachel Robertson. Together with Briggs and Molly, he hurried inside the Carradine mansion.

In the marbled front foyer, Kate stood waiting. With the efficiency of a traffic cop, she directed them. "You two men take over the study. You'll want to spread out those maps and the information from Rachel. Molly, come with me."

Liam wasn't about to be brushed off so easily. Was she playing him? Using him to get what she wanted? If he came right out and asked, would she lie?

He leaned close to her ear and asked, "Is Tom here?"

"No. I already asked Mom. She said that he was staying home today to avoid the reporters."

"We need to talk to him."

She gave him a questioning look. "Is something wrong?"

A lot was wrong. Danger hung ever present around them. He had doubts about the police investigation that seemed to be going nowhere. And even more doubt about their own attempts to investigate. "We should talk to Tom right away."

"I'll put through a call. I can get him to come here." She added, "Jonathan's gone, too. He's in the mountains, at the Cougar Creek development."

"The coward left town," Liam said.

"I think he wants to avoid any negative press on his pet project," she said. "When the going gets tough, the CEO gets gone."

She gave him a little kiss on the cheek and swept Molly toward the back sitting room.

When Liam entered the study, with its wall of untouched books and its aura of quiet, Briggs was completing a call on his cell phone. He turned to Liam. "That was Clauson. It seems that Silverman's Ford Explorer spent some time in a body shop a month ago, for a complete paint and reupholstery job. The guy who worked on it remembered the smell of smoke."

"So Kate's memory of the fire was correct." Liam was relieved. Her remembrance was vindicated by the facts. "Who brought it in?"

"They used Silverman's name and paid in cash." Briggs sat in the leather chair behind the antique desk. "The guy who picked it up fits the description Kate gave to the cops of the professional assassin who attacked at her house. He was wearing golfing gloves."

"Fast work by the cops," Liam said.

"They started with the upscale shops. The kind of place where the Carradines take their cars."

Liam wasn't surprised, since his list of possible suspects were all people close to Kate.

The problem was that they were all high-profile individuals with a lot of money and influence. Investigating them was a nightmare. If Clauson started putting on pressure, these suspects would be quickly lawyered up, safely cocooned by their wealth.

"You know," Briggs said, "you're not doing Kate any favors by withholding information. Somebody wants her dead. The longer the police go without an arrest, the more desperate the attacks are going to become."

"How fast do you think the police would arrest somebody associated with this family?"

"If they've committed a crime—"

"Come off it, Briggs. These people aren't like your average criminals. And this isn't an ordinary crime. Hell, there isn't even a body. Do you really think Clauson can waltz through that marble entryway and slap the cuffs on somebody in this house?"

"Who did you have in mind?"

"I don't know." He cracked open the financial data handed over by Rachel Robertson. "Let's start sifting through this stuff. If we're lucky, we might actually find evidence."

After half an hour of studying the outlines of operational expenses, income and expenditures for three different homeless shelters, Liam saw no red flags. Everything had been carefully detailed, balanced and audited. This information was useless when taken out of context. What had Mickey wanted to show them?

His mood lightened when Kate whisked through the door into the study. In her delicate sandals, her step was graceful. Her expression, guileless. She looked like a breath of pure, fresh air. How could he think that she was using him?

She beamed at Briggs. "Molly is fabulous."

"She's not bad," he said.

"Not bad? She's überorganized. All the details are under control, and my mother adores her."

Liam grumbled, "Things aren't going so well in here."

She circled the desk to stand beside him. When she got close, there was still a tantalizing hint of her perfume. Subtly, she rubbed her arm against his. "What's the problem?"

"This information from Rachel only shows that she's a conscientious administrator. By itself, it has no relevance," Liam said. "Check your cell phone, Kate. See if Mickey tried to call."

She removed her cell from her jeans pocket and scrolled through the message display. "Nothing from Mickey."

Liam stared down at the pages of the financial statements—neat little numbers all in a row. They had to mean something. "Somehow, Rachel's accounting documents are linked with Wayne Silverman. His motives. His plans."

Kate shook her head. "I'm sure Wayne had nothing to do with these accounts. His law firm is exclusive and expensive. They wouldn't be doing work for Rachel Robertson's nonprofit homeless shelters."

"The connection has to be RMS," Liam said. "Wayne is involved in doing the audits for RMS. And the charitable side of your family's business donates a boatload of money to this cause."

"So we need RMS accounting data, for comparison." She flipped open her cell phone again. "No problem."

As she strolled away from the desk, he admired her confident gait. She stood at the bay window, talking on her cell and gazing out at the landscaping. Her upraised hand rested on the polished oak of the window frame. Her profile reflected palely in the glass. She was a part of this house, this world.

He caught only a few words of her conversation. "…printout on fund-raisers. Profit and loss…" Her lips pulled back from her pearly-white teeth in a grin. "…immediately, if not sooner. By fax…" She leaned against the frame. Her back arched slightly. Her breasts lifted.

He wanted to make love to her. Here and now. To sweep all the papers off the desk and claim her. He was sick and tired of piecing together an investigation without all the facts, going against the directions of the police, against Briggs's advice.

All he wanted was to be alone with Kate. Without bodyguards. Without the threat of attack from vandals or assassins. They'd be a hell of a lot better off if he could take her back to the mountains, where she'd be safe.

Briggs stepped away from the desk to greet Peter Rowe, who had glided into the study. "Gentlemen," he said, raising a tumbler filled with amber liquid. "A drink?"

Both Briggs and Liam refused. Liam moved in front of the desk, blocking Peter's view of the documents. If he saw this information, he might know where they were headed with their investigation.

Though Kate believed that Peter was blissfully happy with her mother, Liam considered him to be suspicious. Especially if money was involved. Peter's cash flow depended on Elizabeth. He might be greedy, might want more of his own.

"I hope I'm not interrupting," Peter said.

"It's your house," Liam responded ungraciously.

Peter's ready smile didn't reach his eyes. "I came in here to escape from the world of caterers and florists."

"I thought you took an interest in the charitable side of RMS," Liam said. He was thinking of the necklace, and Peter's supposed trip to the jeweler. How could he work around to that topic? "The fancy dress balls."

"I take a certain satisfaction in escorting my lovely wife." Peter sipped his drink. "By the way, Mr. Briggs, your Molly is quite the organizational whiz. Watch out or we'll hire her away from you."

"About the summer gala," Liam said. There had to be some subtle way to ask about the necklace. "What do you wear to something like that?"

"A tux," Peter said. "That's proper attire for a black-tie event."

"And there's all the stuff that goes with a tux. Like cuff links. Diamond cuff links."

"Perhaps," Peter said.

Obviously, Liam had lost his touch for interrogation. He never stammered around like this when he'd worked for the D.A.'s office. Back then, he had the authority to ask questions. Now, he was some kind of weird, amateur sleuth. Hercule Poirot in Levi's.

He tried again. "Will Elizabeth be wearing her diamonds?"

Peter exchanged a look with Briggs. Then both men looked at Liam. Dryly, Peter questioned, "Her diamonds?"

"You know," Liam continued, digging himself in deeper, "like earrings or a bracelet or—"

"Hey!" Kate had finished her phone call and joined the three men. "What are we talking about?"

"I'm not quite sure," Peter said. "Liam seems to have developed an interest in accessories for formal events."

"Will you excuse us for a moment?"

She linked her arm with Liam's and pulled him into the hallway. She whispered, "What are you doing?"

"I was working up to asking Peter about the necklace. Not very smoothly." He shrugged. "Who were you talking to on the phone?"

"The chief financial officer of RMS. He's faxing me the documents." She directed him through the house, toward the backyard. "Liam, I want to get away from here. There's too much going on. I can't think. If I can't concentrate, my memory is never going to come back."

They stepped outside. As soon as the sun hit his face, Liam's brain cleared. He inhaled a deep breath of fresh air.

She glanced over her shoulder at the house. "It feels like I'm being watched every second."

"That might be because of me." He linked his hand with hers as they strolled toward the gazebo. "I can't take my eyes off you."

"That's different." She lifted her chin, ready for a kiss. "I like having attention from you."

Before he could kiss her, Liam heard a thump and a muffled groan. "What was that?"

The sound was coming from the gazebo. Liam drew the pistol from his ankle holster before charging up the three steps into the filigreed structure.

Mickey lay against the far side. His hands were bound behind his back. He was gagged, and his face was raw and red. He'd been beaten.

Liam knelt beside him and pulled the gag out of his mouth.

Gasping, Mickey said, "Stanhope Jeweler."

Then he passed out.

Chapter Sixteen

This wasn't the first time Kate had knelt beside a man who was close to death.

She held Mickey's hand and stared down into his poor, battered face. His left eye was swollen shut. Discolored, grotesque bruises distorted his forehead and nose. The flesh below his left cheek was slashed and bloody. His mouth hung slack. His breathing was shallow, but he was still alive.

"Don't die," she whispered. "Please don't die."

With a tissue, she wiped at the blood on his face. She squeezed his hand and waited, hoping that he would squeeze back.

Nothing. No response.

She heard the ambulance siren. Paramedics rushed into the yard, to the gazebo, and Kate felt herself being pulled away from Mickey. She stepped back, down the stairs. Her hands were red with blood. Her coral shirt was smeared with indelible stains.

As she stood and watched, the shock of finding Mickey sank into her bones. She was cold. Though Liam held her against his warm body, Kate's chill came from inside, spreading from her heart, turning her to ice. She didn't dare feel anything.

The paramedics tucked the injured man onto a gurney and placed an oxygen mask over his mouth. Wrapped in a blanket, Mickey looked very small, almost childlike. At this moment, she would have given anything to hear his brash voice, to see him reach up to frame a ridiculous headline.

The team from the ambulance left the yard. Mickey was gone, on his way to the hospital.

"There's nothing else we can do for him," Liam said.

"It's my fault," she whispered. "I never should have encouraged him."

"He made his own choices."

"Not this." He hadn't chosen to be beaten. Mickey Wheaton was harmless as a fly. He didn't deserve this fate.

She placed her hand on her breast. Her heart raced. Her blood pounded. But she was still frozen. The warmth of the late afternoon sun failed to penetrate the ice that encased her—freezing her terror, her anger, her sorrow in a glacial veneer. If all those emotions broke free, she would shatter into a million pieces.

How had this happened? Things had seemed to be going well. She and Liam had the beginnings of a wonderful relationship. Kate was back to work with her mother, planning the summer gala. She'd convinced herself that everything was going to be all right, even if she didn't regain her memory.

And now? The threat of danger was a reality. Mickey Wheaton had been beaten within an inch of his life.

Liam guided her back toward the house, where Adam Briggs and Molly stood by, ready to help. They spoke to her, but Kate couldn't decipher their words. Liam's voice was the only sound she heard.

"Come with me," he said. "I need to clean you up a little bit."

Numbly, she followed him into the downstairs bathroom. Liam closed the door.

Kate braced her arms on the sink and stared down at the gold faucets. When Liam turned on the water, she held her hands beneath the spray, washing off Mickey Wheaton's blood.

Using one of her mother's embroidered guest towels, he wiped warm water across her forehead and her cheeks. His hands rubbed her arms, encouraging circulation.

"Kate." Though he stood less than a foot away, he called to her. His voice resonated against the tiled walls. "Can you hear me?"

"Yes."

"Talk to me."

What could she possibly say? She looked up at him—the only person in the world who she could trust. "Liam, when is this going to stop?"

"Now," he said. "It stops now."

"If only that were true." She turned away from him, confronting her reflection in the mirror. Her complexion was ashen. Stark horror etched the lines of her face. She was near the breaking point; she couldn't take any more.

"Listen to me." He tightened his grasp on her arm. "Kate, are you listening?"

"Leave me alone." She wrenched away from him. "Damn it. Get your hands off me."

"That's the spirit," he said. "Let's see another flash of that legendary temper."

"You want me to be angry?"

"To be conscious." He snapped his fingers in front of her eyes. "Wake up. Focus."

She slapped his hand away and blinked. Visual details became more clear. Her fingertips tingled as the ice inside her began to melt. "What difference does it make if I'm focused?"

"You need to be sharp. Intense."

"Why? Why bother?" Her words spewed in a torrent. "Mickey was sharp. He was clever, and look what happened to him. There's no way I'm going to be safe. Not here. There's no real protection. It's only a matter of time before whoever attacked Mickey comes after me. And you. They'll keep coming and coming. We can't get away from them."

"You're right," he said. "You aren't safe here. That's why I'm taking you away. We're going back to the mountains."

A startled cry escaped her lips. Her blood warmed in her veins. "Can we do that?"

"Up to now, I've played inside the guidelines. I went along with the press conference, kept you in town the way Clauson wanted, obeyed the bodyguards. All along, I believed—in my gut—that we had to get away from here."

"To hide?" That had been her first instinct when threatened—hide from the hunters.

"To gather our strength and to fight. On our own terms." A gleam flashed in his hazel eyes. He held both her hands, fusing his determination into her. "I'm not going to wait around. I'd like to check out the jeweler Mickey mentioned, but that's got to come later. We're leaving."

"But how?" She was feeling stronger by the second. Taking action—any kind of action—was better than being helpless and afraid.

"We'll say that we're going to your house. Right now. Borrow one of your mother's cars."

"Impossible." She shook her head. "We'll never get away from the reporters."

"Sure, we will." His absolute confidence gave her reason to hope. "Because we have a secret weapon."

"What's that?"

A slow smile spread across his handsome face. "You're going to drive."

"Me?"

"You're an ace, trained by the pros. I saw how you maneuvered in my clunky Land Rover. Imagine what you could do with—"

"My mother's Mercedes," she said.

It was a challenge, but she was up to it. If it meant going back to the wilderness, back to her sanctuary, Kate would drive to hell and back.

OPERATING ON BLIND FAITH that he was doing the right thing, Liam loaded all the information—the records from Rachel Robertson, the RMS financial statements and the maps—into the Mercedes.

His mind was made up. It was necessary to get Kate away from here, to use the same strategy she'd used when she'd fled from whatever trauma had wiped her memory clean. For twenty-eight days, she'd been safe in the wilderness. Her chances for survival were a hell of a lot better in the mountains. She needed to be away from the constant attacks, the ever-present threat of danger.

She slipped into the driver's seat and fastened her safety belt. Her hands on the steering wheel were steady. When she gazed at him, he saw a sense of purpose in her eyes, not fear.

"You're strong enough to do this," he said.

"You bet I am." Unsmiling, she stuck a pair of Ray•Ban sunglasses on her nose. "Where to?"

"Make sure nobody is following us. Lose the pack, and I'll tell you then."

She hit the garage-door opener. The powerful engine in the Mercedes-Benz purred as they circled the drive in front of her mother's house. Delicately, Kate wended her way through news vans, camera flashes and police patrol cars.

Predictably, several cars followed, forming a parade line.

"I have an extra advantage," she said. "I grew up here. I know the roads."

"Show me."

He was glad to be wearing a seat belt as she whipped a left. The engine roared as she fishtailed up a winding incline, to a stretch of dirt road where there were no houses. Dried weeds on either side of the road blurred as she raced along the road.

In the side mirror, he could see the other cars falling back. "You're doing good."

"I haven't even started."

Her jaw was set. Her gaze, steadfast. And Liam knew he'd done the right thing. This was the Kate Carradine who was capable of fighting the odds. With bloodstains on her shirt and fire in her belly, this woman was ready to kick ass and take no prisoners.

Her route through the foothills and back toward town was so circuitous that he couldn't attempt to follow it. They ended up alone on a side street, with Kate driving at a safe speed. A main thoroughfare was up ahead. Then the highway.

"Go west," he said. "There's an airfield past Morrison."

"We're flying? Why not just take the car?"

Liam had planned their escape route. "When the news teams realize they've lost you, they'll call in other resources to search. Choppers."

"You're right. Damn it!"

"I got it covered," he said. "I already made arrangements with a pilot friend."

"When?"

"I set this up yesterday, before Clauson ordered us to stay in town," he said. "We're going to fly away in our own little chopper."

"Do you know how to fly a helicopter?"

"I'm certified, and this one is easy to fly. The downside is that I've got to pay this guy top dollar for his time and his machine. This trip is going to cost a small fortune."

"Worth every penny," she said.

They left the Mercedes at the airfield and boarded the tiny helicopter. Though capable of holding a pilot and three passengers, it was tiny inside. In the cockpit, Liam donned a headset with a speaker. Kate was outfitted with the same equipment so they could talk to each other over the whir of the rotors.

With a wave to his charter-pilot buddy, Liam lifted off. The foothills receded as they climbed into a sunset-colored sky. He aimed west, toward clouds of magenta with gold underbellies. The flight plan he had filed was for Vail, which was not, of course, their real destination.

Swooping through the air, exhilaration raced through him. They were free. Up here, no one could touch them.

"I love this," Kate said through the headset. "Are these little rotor guys hard to fly?"

"I could teach you, but not right now." There were

other things to discuss. "Did you ever reach your step-brother on the phone?"

"He wasn't answering."

"Do you think Tom was responsible for the attack on Mickey?"

"Why? If Tom and Wayne were friends with Mickey, they were all on the same side."

"Not if Mickey threatened to expose whatever Tom was doing."

"A beating isn't Tom's style," she said. "He likes guns."

Liam didn't think any of their upper-class suspects would get their hands dirty in a slugfest. "He could have hired someone. Like those jackasses who came to my cabin."

"If they wanted to keep Mickey quiet, why leave him alive?"

A beating was an intimidation tactic, a warning to Mickey to keep his mouth shut. The little reporter had discovered damaging evidence. Or he might have known all along.

Mickey, Wayne Silverman and Tom might have started out as a three-way partnership. But what had their initial plan been? Embezzlement? Blackmail?

Liam had to believe the answers would be found when they compared the documents from RMS with Rachel Robertson's reports.

After the chopper reached appropriate altitude, he veered north toward Grand Lake. From his years as a charter pilot, he knew the terrain by landmarks. There was only about an hour of sunlight left. It should be enough time to reach his cabin.

"We're on the run," she said. "This feels like what happened to me before. Someone else was savagely attacked, but I escaped."

"Are you remembering?"

"Nothing specific. The feeling is similar, but I'm not so confused this time." He felt her hand on his arm, and turned toward her. She planted a sweet, lingering kiss on his mouth. "I'm not scared, Liam. Because you're with me."

He hoped her faith in him was justified. His decision to run would surely infuriate the police, the Carradines and Adam Briggs. He couldn't count on friendly support from anybody.

It was just him and Kate against the world.

As he flew at the edge of sunset, he felt good. This was the way it was supposed to be.

AFTER A BRIEF STOP AT his cabin, to pick up camping supplies and food, Liam directed the chopper toward her former campsite—the place where he first saw Rain. It was extremely fortunate that he hadn't divulged the exact location of her hideout. He could have done so. At his cabin were the aerial photographs he'd used to find Kate.

Clauson knew about the photos. The local sheriff could put together a search-and-rescue team to pinpoint their location within a few square miles. "We can't stay here for long, Kate."

"Why not?"

"If the police decide to search, they have an idea of our approximate location."

"We could find another hideout," she said. "I'm good at this."

"We're not going into hiding. We're tracking."

"We're the hunters," she said. "I like that."

Dusk had settled. If Liam hadn't flown this route before, he never would have found the spot. It took only a
few passes across the wooded hillsides to locate the open
field near her cave.

They touched down. The blades went silent. Night's
shadows spread across the land.

Kate was delighted, ecstatic. She leaped from the
chopper with a triumphant whoop. "We're here!"

Even in her sandals, she was sure-footed. In the soft
illumination of early starlight, she danced across the
meadow. Her movements were wild, primitive and free.
She was the spirit of the forests. She was Rain.

His heart beat faster as he watched her. There were
practical tasks that needed to be attended to—unpacking
supplies, preparing food, camouflaging the chopper. But
he was driven toward her.

Nothing else mattered. He grabbed a sleeping bag and
joined her in the field.

Her delighted laughter rippled like clear rapids in a
stream. When she caught hold of his hand, he felt the primal energy of the earth.

He pulled her into his arms for a long, deep kiss.

She met his passion with her own fierce need. Her caresses aroused him. She tore open his shirt, trailing kisses
across his chest.

He unbuttoned her bloodstained blouse. Underneath,
she wore a white lace camisole. Her taut nipples peaked
against the delicate material.

"Very pretty," he said. "Matching panties?"

"Of course." She peeled off her jeans and stood before
him. Her undergarments were sultry sophistication, even
sexier in the wilderness.

Moonlight unfurled across the meadow as he spread

out the sleeping bag amid sweetgrass and fragrant mint. In the vast stillness of a mountain night, surrounded by forests and rugged cliffs, they could have been the only man and woman in the world.

She knelt in the center of the sleeping bag. Smiling up at him, she looked like a wood nymph.

"I want to remember this forever," she said. "This night. This freedom. And you."

Kate opened her arms to him. When he joined her on the sleeping bag, she opened her heart. The breeze sang in her ears, gently gliding across her naked shoulders and refreshing the heat of her desire. Pure delight filled her. She had never been so happy.

Their lovemaking took on the scents and sounds of the forest. Perfectly natural. Perfectly sensual. Perfect.

He stroked between her thighs. His skillful fingers teased her toward fulfillment. He lifted her camisole, caressed her breasts and her tight nipples. When his mouth joined again with hers, she welcomed his tongue.

He struggled for a moment, digging through the pockets of his discarded jeans for his wallet. "I need a condom," he said.

"For carrying water," she said, reminding him of the survival use for condoms.

"For keeping you safe," he said. "That's all I've ever wanted. To protect you."

He entered her quickly, and she spread her legs wide, taking him into her body, opening herself to the galaxies of stars that spread across the velvet skies. At one with the universe, she responded to his hard thrusts. She succumbed to the shivering, spectacular pleasure he gave her.

Liam collapsed beside her, snuggled close on the narrow sleeping bag. "A night to remember."

She hoped it was only one night of many—an eternity of nights in his arms.

Purely contented, she sighed. It would have been lovely to disregard the dangers present in the outside world, but she knew better. They couldn't hide forever. They had to find the truth.

In his arms, she wiggled until she was face-to-face with him. Teasing, she caught his earlobe between her teeth and tugged. Then, she whispered, "Would you like to see fifty thousand in cash and a small fortune in diamonds?"

Chapter Seventeen

With an armload of camping supplies, Kate and Liam hiked up the incline to her cave behind the boulders. Though she had a sentimental attachment to this place where she'd lived for twenty-eight days, she wasn't disappointed to find that her tidy campsite didn't look the same as when she'd left. The indigenous wildlife—squirrels, deer and birds—had rummaged through her hideout like curious neighbors peeking into a deserted house.

The spit across her fire pit had fallen down. Her woven plates were scattered, and her well-swept dirt floor was scattered with pine needles and leaves. Nature had already begun to reclaim this place. Within one season, she suspected there would be little trace of her habitation.

She picked up the woven basket she had filled with stones, one for each day of hiding. She would take this back to Denver as a reminder. Twenty-eight days of wilderness sanctuary. Twenty-eight days that had changed her life.

Liam spread out their supplies and lit up a Coleman lantern.

"Too bright," she said, shielding her eyes.

"We're going to need light. We have work to do tonight."

Though she agreed, Kate would much rather spend their night in the mountains in more pleasurable endeavors. Making love in the starlight. Reveling in the silence. Being part of the forest.

Apparently, Liam had a different agenda. He pointed into her shallow cave and said, "Show me the money."

The farthest point in her cave was only twelve feet from the opening. She crawled inside, removed the rocks she'd piled over the cache and took out the bundle wrapped in an old T-shirt.

Feeling like a squirrel who had just raided her own storehouse, she brought the treasure to Liam, who sat just inside the cave's opening.

He unwrapped the T-shirt. Neatly banded bundles of hundred-dollar bills fell on the dirt cave floor.

"Damn," he said. "This is craziness."

She opened the pouch containing the jewelry and removed two diamond tennis bracelets and a flashy gold-and-diamond necklace.

"I still don't remember this piece," she said. The design of the necklace was relatively simple—a choker with three strands of diamonds. At the center was a larger stone in an emerald cut. Even without a jeweler's loupe, Kate could tell that the centerpiece diamond wasn't of the highest quality.

"What do you think it's worth?" Liam asked.

"Hard to guess. There's a lot of ice. Probably several thousand dollars."

"And you don't remember your mother wearing this necklace?"

"It must be new. Maybe it was a recent gift from Peter." She dangled the sparkling gems from her fingers. "This style seems like something he'd choose. A lot of flash. But the centerpiece stone is a bit cloudy."

"It could be that your mother didn't like it."

"Entirely possible," she said. "Elizabeth prefers quality to excessive display. She'd rather have one perfect diamond on a simple chain."

"Tomorrow, we'll find out if the necklace belonged to her."

"How?"

"I hate to bring this up." His eyes were tinged with regret. "It's about Mickey. He said two words before he passed out. Stanhope Jeweler."

The reminder of Mickey and the beating he'd taken sent a shiver down her spine. It was awful to think that these jewels might have caused that attack. Even worse, this treasure might have played a part in Wayne Silverman's death.

Seen in that context, the diamonds seemed ugly to her. She dropped the necklace back into the pouch. "My family has done business with Stanhope before. They'll talk to me."

Liam reached toward her. His hand rested on her knee. "We'll figure this out. The next time, when you go back to town, you won't have to worry about danger. You'll be safe."

"Being here like this…" Her words trailed off in a wistful sigh. She leaned her back against the cave wall. "I almost wish I didn't have to go back."

"You'd be bored if you stayed in the mountains," he said. "I've seen you in action. The social events, RMS and the charity stuff. Not to mention the makeovers, the stylists and the manicures."

"Is it really that much?"

"You're in a constant whirlwind," he said. "It's who you are."

"I'd rather be Rain."

In Liam's hazel eyes, she saw confirmation that he wished for the same thing. He cared about Rain—more than he could about Kate Carradine. She said, "You like that part of me."

"I do," he said. "A basic, uncomplicated woman. Purely natural."

Gently, his hand stroked her cheek. His fingers traced the outline of her chin and her lips. "Beautiful," he said.

She remembered the first time he'd told her that he liked the way she looked. Rather, he liked the way Rain looked.

His hand glided down her shoulder, and he straightened the zipper on the oversize sweatshirt she wore for warmth. "A strong woman," he said. "Pretty and smart and—"

"Stop it," she muttered. "I'm starting to feel jealous."

"Of yourself?"

"Of the woman I can never really be."

As Rain, she was a free spirit with no past and no responsibilities beyond simple survival. As Rain, she wasn't embarrassed to dance in a mountain meadow and celebrate the moonlight.

Truly, that was a part of her. But not her whole life. Rain was also limited, just as a child who knew nothing more of her surroundings than the immediate sights and sounds.

After a while, Rain's lifestyle would become tedious. Kate Carradine was far too jaded and experienced to live in a wonderland of innocence.

She pointed to the folders he'd carried with them. "Let's get started."

Since Liam had already studied the documents from

Rachel Robertson, he kept those spreadsheets. Kate had the financial printouts from RMS. "What are we looking for?" she asked.

"Evidence of embezzlement. That seems like the most obvious crime."

"Too obvious." She glared at the neatly organized financial statements. "These numbers are thoroughly checked and audited."

"Wayne Silverman's job," he said. "Overseeing the legal aspects of the audits."

"But he couldn't have tampered with this data. There are invoices, receipts and documentation."

"We'll make a comparison and look for discrepancies," he said. "The link between Rachel's charity and RMS is contributions. I'll read off her deposits from RMS, and you check the RMS documents to see if there's a corresponding donation."

They went through a fiscal year's worth of donations without finding any difference.

Kate wasn't surprised. RMS was a large company, professionally run. Their records had to be accurate. At the same time, she knew that with a multitiered, complex system, there were also possibilities for error.

Liam sat opposite her in the cave. His long legs stretched out straight in front of him. She reached over with her bare toes and pushed against the scuffed soles of his boots.

He glanced up from his scrutiny of the pages. "What is it?"

"We need to be more imaginative," she said. "Why would Mickey have wanted us to look at these documents?"

"Numbers are numbers, Kate. They don't lie."

"But they might be hiding something."

"Like what?"

She tucked her bare feet underneath her. With both hands, she formed a headline. It was Mickey's favorite gesture. "Ten billion dollars," she said.

She dropped her hands. In a quiet voice, she added, "Eleven thousand."

"I get it," he said. "Throw out a huge number, and the smaller amount seems insignificant."

More than anyone else at RMS, Kate was aware of the vast expenditures involved in putting together a charity event. For something huge, like the summer gala and silent auction, there were expenses that ranged from the rental of a ballroom at the exclusive Brown Palace Hotel to tips for valet parking.

"Here's what we need to look for," she said. "What were Rachel's expenses for last year's summer gala?"

"Why would she have any costs? This is supposed to work to her benefit."

"And it does," Kate said. "But there are always expenses."

Liam peered at the numbers. "Invitations. Printing. Thank-you gifts. A luncheon for her board of directors. She paid for framing some artwork. Some flowers. You're right—this stuff adds up. Roughly, the total is about two thousand."

Kate scanned her own sheet. "Exactly $2,174.21. That's the amount RMS cut her a check for."

Liam scanned the pages once, then again. "I don't see it. Rachel never recorded that check."

"Because she never received it," Kate said triumphantly. "And, of course, she never mentioned the amount to me. RMS donated over a hundred grand. She wasn't going to quibble about a couple thou."

"So let's assume Wayne Silverman discovered this discrepancy," Liam said. "What difference would it make? This seems like such a piddling amount."

"The tip of the iceberg," she said.

Kate slid her finger down the page. She found double payments for uniforms for a softball league, and a check to a florist who she knew had donated his services.

If she went through all the accounting for all the various charities RMS supported, the siphoning off of cash in small amounts would add up to a very healthy total. "And I know who's doing it," she said.

A clear picture formed in her mind. Her mother generally took responsibility for presenting the donation checks to the various charities. In the case of a large donation, Elizabeth's visit was a public-relations event. Photographs were taken of Elizabeth Carradine shaking hands and smiling as she handed over a check.

Always at her mother's side was Peter Rowe. He flashed his photogenic smile for the camera, and he handled the checks so Elizabeth wouldn't have to be bothered.

"It's Peter," she said.

"I hate to poke holes in this theory," he said. "But wouldn't the checks be made out to the charities?"

"Not necessarily. Some of the contributions—especially those considered to be petty cash—come from the family's personal funds. It's a tax write-off for the Carradines. If we were legal auditors, like Wayne, we could nail down this evidence."

"You're right. It's Peter Rowe. He's the embezzler." Liam's fingers drew into a fist. "And we've got him."

Finally, they had evidence that could be verified, penny by penny. Her stepfather had been stealing from

RMS and the charities the family funded. "In his legal capacity, Wayne must have found out," she said. "Like we did. Then, Wayne set out to blackmail my stepfather."

"You're brilliant, Kate."

She smiled at him and winked. "I know."

"We can speculate about what happened next. But we'll never know for sure unless Peter decides to confess."

"Let's speculate." She scooted across the cave and sat beside him. "I like being brilliant."

Liam draped his arm around her shoulders in a casual, comfortable gesture. Together, they worked out a scenario. When Wayne had brought her to the mountains, supposedly for a camping trip, he'd expected to receive a blackmail payment from Peter Rowe. Peter had delivered the cash and the jewels, and Wayne had loaded it all in his backpack. Then Peter had changed his mind.

"Maybe Wayne got greedy," she said. "Maybe he asked for more money."

"The downfall of all blackmailers," Liam said. "And Peter shot him."

"That still doesn't explain one important detail," she said. "Why did Wayne bring me along?"

"He wanted a witness," Liam suggested. "Wayne figured that your stepfather would never do anything to harm him if you were waiting in the car."

She frowned. That explanation didn't quite ring true. Her involvement was more complicated than merely being a witness. Had she plotted this whole scheme with Wayne Silverman? Not possible!

But her long-term memory had pretty much returned, and she couldn't remember discussing blackmail. Besides, Kate knew in her heart that she would never go along with a plan that took money away from the charities she loved. She wouldn't want to hurt RMS. Or her mother. Poor Elizabeth! She'd be devastated to know that her husband was a criminal.

Kate leaned her head on Liam's shoulder. Had they figured it out correctly? Was this the final solution? Somehow, it seemed too easy. She didn't think they'd taken everything into account. And they didn't really have proof that Peter had murdered Wayne Silverman.

Bottom line: they'd never know the whole truth until her memory returned.

THE NEXT MORNING, LIAM DIDN'T want to open his eyes. Inside a double sleeping bag, he was snuggled with Kate. Their legs entwined. Her sensuous, slender body pressed against him, and he wished he could nest here forever. Safe and quiet. The mountains were his true home. His heart was here. *I don't want to get up. Don't want to leave.*

Because, he suspected, today was going to be a bitch.

Though they'd figured out one big piece of the puzzle, their investigation wasn't over by a long shot. While they had the chopper, he wanted to fly over possible areas where Kate might have seen the fire, in the hopes that her memory might kick in. Then, there were phone calls to make. Lots of angry people to talk to, notably Detective Clauson, who could follow up on their embezzlement theory.

Liam exhaled slowly. If they were right about blackmail and murder, Clauson could make an arrest and Kate would be safe.

But he didn't want to take her back to her world. He

wanted to keep his natural woman hidden away with him in the mountain wilderness.

She wiggled around beside him, and he felt her mouth nuzzling below his chin.

"No," he murmured. "I don't want to wake up."

She kissed his cheek. "It's a beautiful dawn. All pink and moist."

"Like you." He glided his hand down her back and cupped her firm, rounded butt. "Let's stay here."

"I'd like that," she said. "But I think a search party might notice the helicopter parked in the field."

Reluctantly, he opened his eyes.

She was about six inches away from his face. She cocked her head to one side, then the other, then she leaned in and kissed his nose.

"You're chipper this morning," he said.

"I'm brilliant. You said so yourself."

Brilliant and sexy. He pulled her close and gave her a real wake-up kiss.

The teasing went out of her, replaced by a different sort of tension. She wrapped her legs around him. Her body rubbed against his.

Liam enfolded her in his arms. Waking up wasn't so bad, after all.

AFTER THEY'D HAD COFFEE made on the Coleman stove and loaded their gear into the chopper, it was still early morning—a little before eight o'clock. Liam tossed her the cell phone. "Try calling your stepbrother."

"Tom won't be awake." She flipped open the phone and studied the display. "No signal."

He'd suspected as much. They were in a remote area, surrounded by high cliffs. "We'll try him later."

"What will I tell him?" Sarcastically, she said, "Oh, Tom, by the way, your father is an embezzler. And probably a psycho murderer."

"You had the memory about Tom," Liam pointed out. "You said that Tom knew. Maybe he's got evidence, something that points clearly to Peter."

"Even if he does," she said, "Tom won't betray his father. They're pretty close."

"And Peter pays all his bills," Liam said.

"God, you're cynical."

"It's the truth, isn't it?"

"I suppose it is. Tom doesn't have a real job, but he gets paid by RMS. Through Peter. I guess Tom is a glorified gofer." She frowned. "I'm not like that, am I?"

How could she even ask? "You're the one who gives the orders. Not the one who takes them."

"Right," she said, nodding toward the chopper. "Let's fly."

Last night, he'd gone over the maps Molly had gathered for him. He'd located her campsite, then drawn a circle around it, encompassing the areas where there had been forest fires. The resulting quadrant was fairly good sized.

If he'd had a third point of reference, he might have triangulated the map to a more specific area. As it was, they'd be searching more square miles than he cared to calculate.

When they were airborne, he handed the maps over to her. "I divided up the map like the spokes of a wheel. We'll start in this area."

"And what am I supposed to do?"

"See if anything looks familiar. A road. Or a landmark. If not, cross off the area."

He didn't have a lot of confidence in this method. The

view from the air was different than on the ground. But they might as well take this tour. Maybe they'd get lucky and some sight would jar her memory.

They neared one of the burned areas, and he dropped down to give her a closer look.

"My God," she whispered. "It's terrible."

The earth below was devastated, blackened and barren. A few charred trees stood in mute testament.

The pattern of destruction showed the efforts of firefighters. One hillside was wiped out. Another seemed untouched.

"Does anything look familiar?" he asked.

"I can't tell. When I was here, there was a forest. And flames. Now it's all dead."

They had cycled through about a quarter of the area when Liam decided they should try again with their phone calls. He landed the chopper on a hillside and took out the cell phone.

"I got a signal," he said. "I'll call CCC."

And he hoped that Molly would answer. She'd be sympathetic.

No such luck. It was Briggs. He wasted no time on subtlety. "Get your butt back here, Liam. And do it now."

"That's not going to happen. Not while Kate's in danger."

"You've completely screwed up Clauson's investigation. Instead of solving a missing-person case, the police and about ten thousand reporters are occupied with searching for you and Kate."

"They can call off the search. We're fine," Liam said. "How's Mickey doing?"

"He's been upgraded to serious condition, but he hasn't regained consciousness."

"Listen, Briggs. Kate and I have new evidence. Financial statements indicate someone was embezzling from RMS. Wayne Silverman was a legal auditor. He might have discovered the crime."

"Great," he said gruffly. "Now get back here. Let me know where you'll be and I'll have bodyguards waiting."

It seemed like a rational plan, but Liam wasn't ready to give up. Not quite yet. "I'll call you before we return to Denver. It'll be today."

He disconnected the call and handed the phone to Kate. "Give Stanhope Jeweler a try."

She leaned against the chopper while she made her call. The wind rustled through her short hair, and the August sunlight played on her face. She looked great even though she was wearing one of his T-shirts, which was extra voluminous on her slender frame.

He ought to take her back to town and allow the bodyguards from CCC to protect her. After they turned over their evidence to Clauson, his investigation would go on high speed. He could take Peter into custody and…

"Damn!" Kate shouted as she ended her phone call and stalked toward him.

"What's wrong?" he asked. "Wouldn't Stanhope Jeweler give you information?"

"Oh, they told me it was my mother's necklace," she said. "I described it and the jeweler verified making a copy. We were right. It was a gift from Peter."

"Then what's the problem?"

She removed her sunglasses and peered up at him. "It wasn't Peter who requested the copy. It was Tom."

Chapter Eighteen

Frustrated by another surprising shift in their investigation, Kate collapsed against Liam and burrowed her face into his chest. The solution they'd so carefully hammered out last night had twisted back into a question. Why Tom? Why had he wanted a copy of her mother's diamond necklace?

"We're never going to figure out the crime," she said, "much less who did it."

"It's still embezzlement," he said. "Tom must have had access to RMS checks. Therefore, he's our embezzler."

"I never thought he had that much ambition." It was also hard for her to believe that Tom would betray his father. She groaned. "I want this to be over."

He stroked her back and shoulders—an unthinking gesture that was strangely comforting because of its casual nature. Their relationship was about more than passion. They were friends, companions, equals.

He said, "When you think about it, Tom actually has a better motive."

"How do you figure?"

"As you've said before, your stepfather doesn't need the money. Even if he divorced your mother, he'd be well-paid. But Tom? His connection to the Carradine fortune is more tenuous."

That was true. Though Tom was involved in RMS board meetings as a representative of her stepfather, he'd never really been part of the family business. Her stepbrother had no real power.

"One thing bothers me," Liam said. "Why did Mickey lie to us?"

She'd been so focused on Tom's potential guilt that she hadn't even considered Mickey's part. "Maybe Mickey was protecting Tom."

"More likely, he was protecting himself."

"How so?"

"We already connected the three of them—Tom, Mickey and Wayne. Suppose they were working together. Embezzling or blackmailing. I'm not sure what the hell they were doing, but their game got rough. Somebody got greedy. And they turned on each other. Wayne was killed."

"And Mickey was beaten."

"Last man standing," Liam said, "is Tom."

"I hate this new scenario." The idea that her stepfather had hired people to kill her was less disturbing than if the threat came from Tom, who had often gone out of his way to support her. "I always thought he was on my side."

"Don't take it too hard." He leaned away from her and tilted her chin up. Gently, he brushed wisps of hair off her forehead. "We're probably wrong about this, too."

She gazed up into his warm, hazel eyes. If he hadn't been with her, she'd have had no one to trust—no one who truly supported her. "The truth still comes down to one thing, doesn't it?"

"Your memory."

Locked inside her head was the real answer. She'd witnessed a murder. She knew who'd killed Wayne. The truth was there, just beyond her grasp.

If she concentrated really hard, she could recreate the images she'd seen before. The blood. The chase. The fire. But nothing more.

She couldn't see the murderer. Tom Rowe? Or Peter? Or even Jonathan? With a shudder, she realized that even Mickey might be a killer. It would explain why he knew so much about her.

"Liam, what if I never remember?"

"You will." He gave her a quick kiss that was utterly unsatisfying. "Let's take another look at the maps. We don't have much fuel left so we need to narrow our search area."

She followed him back to the chopper, where he took the huge map from the forest service and refolded it to show a smaller area. "We haven't flown over this quadrant yet."

Thus far, their aerial search had been unenlightening. She couldn't visualize what things looked like on the ground. "Maybe it would help if you explain the map to me."

The basic pattern of the map was a grid. It included lots of wavy lines, tiny markings and notations that referenced altitude and miles. She didn't get it. The scribbles looked like abstract art—nothing she could mentally translate into real terrain. "Which way is north?"

"Top of the page."

"And right now, in the real world." She stuck out her arm and pointed. "North is that way?"

He took her shoulders and turned her thirty degrees, correcting her aim. "That way."

"My internal compass isn't great," she said.

"Not a problem," he said. "As long as you get where you're going."

Though he didn't come right out and tell her that she was a directionally-challenged moron, she heard a hint of irritation in his voice.

He reached into his shirt pocket for his sunglasses. His eyes were masked, but the tension around his mouth showed his annoyance. Returning to the map, he pointed out squiggly lines that were service roads and notations for cabins.

"In your memory," he said, "when you saw Wayne coming toward you, was there a cabin?"

"I don't know."

"Take your time, Kate. Think about it. Was there a cabin?"

She closed her eyes and concentrated, trying to summon up the vision. How did her memory start? She imagined herself sitting in the passenger side of Wayne's Ford Explorer, looking out the window.

A man came toward her. It was Wayne. He was bleeding from a terrible chest wound.

What else did she see?

Forests. Trees...

Was there a cabin? She couldn't tell, but she heard something, a familiar sound. Her eyes snapped open. "A stream. I think I heard the rushing of a stream."

Liam returned to the map. "We'll assume you and Wayne went to a cabin. It doesn't make sense for you to stop in the forest in the middle of nothing."

"Could have been a campsite," she said. "Or a mobile home."

She wasn't deliberately trying to be difficult, but he

reacted as if she were throwing darts into his stupid map. Didn't he realize that this was at least as frustrating for her as it was for him?

"Right here." He pointed to the map. "This is a cabin. There was a forest fire over here. And this is a stream."

"So what?"

"Focus, Kate. I'm trying to locate a site that fits your memory."

"Then you should stop being so condescending," she said. "Last night, you thought I was brilliant."

"And you are when it comes to planning charity events and gala affairs."

"But I'm not smart enough to read a map?"

He snapped the page taut. "Concentrate. Here's the cabin. There's the fire."

She pointed to a winding line. "What's that?"

"It's the stream." He squinted at the page, reading the tiny print. "Cougar Creek."

She gasped. This couldn't be a coincidence. "Cougar Creek Development. That's Jonathan's pet development project. That cabin must be the hunting lodge, the only existing structure on the property."

It made sense that Wayne had taken her there on their supposed camping trip. He could have told her that there was a bit of business to transact before the weekend. She wouldn't have suspected that anything was amiss. "That has to be where we met the murderer."

Quietly, Liam said, "Jonathan."

"Not necessarily. A lot of people have access to that hunting lodge. Anybody in my family."

"And now? Who's there now?"

"A lot of people. From what I understand, construction on the roads is under way at the site. Jonathan's there, supervising."

"We'll fly over," he said.

"Forget it," she said. Now, she was annoyed. How could she have missed something so simple? "I can't tell anything from the air. We need to go there."

She jabbed her forefinger at the map, harder than she'd intended. It fell from Liam's hands.

"What are you saying, Kate? That we should charge over to Cougar Creek and confront a murderer head-on?"

"Of course not." But she knew they were on the right track. She could feel it in her bones. "We need to follow those service roads leading toward the area where there was a forest fire."

"I'd rather not get any closer than twenty thousand vertical feet." He bent down and picked up the map. "Did you say there's a crew working over there? Putting in roads?"

"I think so. Why?"

"A mountain road crew sounds a lot like the guys who came to my cabin and shot up my plane."

"People who worked for Jonathan," she said. It would be very like her ex-husband to send over his crew to harass her. But to kill her? And how could Jonathan be involved in embezzling from the charity side of RMS's business?

Liam swung open the door on the chopper. "We'll go back to my cabin and get the Jeep."

"What if the police are waiting for us at your cabin?"

"Only one way to find out."

AS THEY BOARDED THE SMALL helicopter and lifted off, Liam considered the irony. His cabin was less than twenty aerial miles away from the Cougar Creek development. So close.

Yet, he'd had no idea the development was there. Why would he? It wasn't his business.

But Kate should have known. Apparently, she was like most people who came to the mountains—unable to visualize what lay beyond the next hill and valley. A bird's-eye view was impossible for her to comprehend.

He knew she wasn't trying to be a pain in the butt, but her attitude was beginning to grate on his nerves. She didn't have the patience for investigating. She didn't understand that all their supposed solutions were only theories until the police verified them and turned their guesses into evidence.

Clauson needed to be involved as soon as possible. Briggs had been correct, and Liam was painfully aware that running off to the mountains wasn't the smartest route he could have taken. He'd acted on instinct instead of calm, rational intellect.

Kate had that effect on him.

He glanced over at her. Beside him in the cockpit, she sat with her arms folded below her breasts. Her body language told him not to talk to her. She was sulking because he hadn't immediately jumped to do her bidding.

"Lighten up," he said into the headset. "If you're right about Cougar Creek, driving on the service roads ought to trigger your memory."

"Maybe," she said. "And maybe not."

"Hey, princess, you got your way. We're doing this your way."

She looked down her nose. "If you're going to be nasty, at least be accurate. I'm not a princess. I'm an heiress."

In spite of his irritation, he had to laugh. No matter which side of her personality was onstage, she was spunky as hell.

He turned away from her and hovered high above his property. There were no cars, no sign of people waiting. In a downward spiral, he descended.

Leaving the chopper parked beside his Super Cub, Liam led her to the battered Jeep parked near the house. He slipped into the driver's seat and cranked the key in the engine. It took three tries before it caught.

The Jeep was an ancient vehicle, only used to plow out the snowdrifts in winter. "Hang on, Kate. This is going to be a bumpy ride."

On the plus side, he thought, bouncing around in the Jeep ought to shake the snotty attitude right out of her.

As they drove past his Cub, she said, "I'm really sorry about your plane. It's my fault that it was shot up."

"You didn't pull the trigger."

He thought back to those moments when they'd been crouched on the hillside, watching the mindless vandalism. In spite of his outrage, his strongest emotion had been to protect her. That instinct had been running his life ever since.

Technically, he hadn't saved her life when he'd found her in the forest. She might have survived for another twenty-eight days. But he had found her. Her safety was his responsibility, and he had welcomed that burden. He had wanted to take care of her.

But now? She didn't need so much protecting. She wasn't Rain. Not anymore. She was Her Imperial Majesty. The Heiress.

They jostled along for a few moments in silence. He took a back road, which was the most direct route toward Cougar Creek.

"I have a thought," she said.

His grip on the steering wheel tightened. He wasn't sure if he wanted to hear her latest idea.

"Suppose," she said, "I buy you a brand new airplane. You could choose whatever you wanted."

Her offer struck him as wrong. "Are you trying to pay me off?"

"Well, I owe you so very much." She sounded brittle. Like her mother. "After everything you've done for me, buying an airplane is the least I can do."

"After everything I've done?" His rear molars ground together. His irritation turned to outright hostility. She was treating him like a bellboy, someone who carried her luggage. "Does that payoff include the sex?"

"There's no need to be angry, Liam. I'll buy you a plane. After all, I can afford it."

"I'll manage." He expected the insurance company would pay for the damage. Or he could get financing. It was his plane, his problem.

"Please," she said. "Let me do this for you."

He hated her attitude. "I don't need for you to step in and start running my life the way you run your charity events."

"Is that what you think?"

"That's right." He wasn't Peter Rowe, her mother's tame lapdog. And he wasn't Jonathan Proctor, marrying his way into top management of RMS.

"You don't want to take my help," she said.

"Don't need it."

"Why not? Because your life is so perfect?"

He didn't have to justify himself to her. Or to anybody else. "Just who the hell do you think you are?"

"I'm Kate Carradine."

"Yeah. That's the problem."

Much as he adored the free spirit of Rain, he couldn't stand the heiress.

THEY RODE IN SILENCE. Behind her sunglasses, Kate fought tears. She couldn't change who she was. Maybe her offer to buy Liam a plane had been insensitive, but she hadn't meant it that way. She was being helpful, giving him something he needed and wanted.

It was probably better that this blowup had happened before their relationship went any further. She should have expected Liam to turn on her. That was the way her life had always been. Mickey had it pegged when he'd said she had poor judgment in men.

Once again, she'd fallen for an overly critical guy who wanted her to be something she clearly was not. He wanted Rain—the wild mountain woman. Never mind that Rain was an aberration, an identity she'd assumed under terrible stress.

It's better this way. She and Liam had no real possibility of a future together. Her responsibilities were in Denver, and he wouldn't fit in. He probably didn't even own a tux.

She dashed away an errant tear. She didn't care about tuxedos, didn't care if he was rough around the edges. She liked his granite jaw. She loved his hard, muscular body. Why couldn't she be Rain for him?

"Look around you," he said. "We're coming onto the forest-service road."

She forced herself to concentrate. More than anything, she wanted this to be over. "How far is it from the development?"

"Judging from the maps, about four miles."

Taking a left turn, he jolted onto a rutted dirt road, little more than a pathway through the surrounding trees. Though he was driving fairly slowly, the tree branches whipped against the sides of the Jeep. "This is it," she said. "This is the road I drove with the Explorer."

"Tell me about it. Talk your way through the memories."

"I was in Wayne's car. Driving." A remembered pain shot through her arm. She reached up and touched the scar where a bullet had torn through her flesh. "I was shot. Wayne was bleeding."

Intense sensory memories raced through her brain. She smelled the forest fire. Sheer terror clenched in her gut. The hunters were after them.

Her head whipped around. She peered through the rear window. She couldn't see them, but she knew they were there.

The Jeep stopped. They had reached the end of the rutted road. She felt Liam's hand on her arm.

"Is this the place?" he asked.

She was breathing hard. *Smoke clogged her lungs. But she couldn't stop now. They had to get away.* "If they catch up to us, we're dead."

"What did you do next?" Liam said.

Fighting her fear, she opened the door to the Jeep. Her hand shook, and her insides trembled. She didn't want to go any farther, but she had to. There was no choice. She had to remember.

She swallowed hard and said, "I had to help Wayne. There was so much blood. I came around to his side of the car and opened it. But he wouldn't get out."

Take the backpack. "He wouldn't go anywhere until I promised to take the backpack."

"With the cash and jewels," Liam said.

"I didn't know. At the time, I didn't know why the backpack was so important. But I couldn't argue with Wayne. He was…"

"He was what?"

"Dying," she said.

Kate pushed her way through the trees blocking the road. Her steps were heavy. She remembered the cumbersome backpack, the weight of Wayne, leaning on her as they trudged forward. They couldn't go back. The hunters were after them.

She stepped out of the forested area. Acres of blackened, devastated land stretched before them. It was a nightmare landscape.

"The fire hadn't come this far," she said.

Flames leaped from tree to tree. The heat blasted her face. She wore her parka to protect her arms.

"This was our only escape," she said. "The hunters wouldn't follow us here. Only a crazy person would walk directly into a forest fire."

"Not crazy," Liam said. "That was smart thinking. It probably saved your life."

She stumbled forward on the charred earth. Grime and soot coated her feet in the sandals. "I could see the edge of the flames. So close."

She pointed downhill. Once there had been a forest. Now, there was only sky.

The earth beneath her feet was marshy. The grass grew high. She saw beaver ponds. An aching cough rattled in her throat.

"Here," she said. "We went this way."

Down the gently sloping hillside, she walked slowly, remembering what had been here before. Beaver ponds.

A lot more water. Wetlands. Now, the stream, which was still blocked and diverted by the burned remnants of beaver lodges, broke into several paths. The water spread like trickling fingers, massaging the earth, encouraging growth. A bit of green lichen at the edge of the stream gave her hope.

She squatted down and touched the fragile growth. "Everything is going to be all right. We're going to make it."

She'd said those words to Wayne.

He coughed uncontrollably. His strength was at an end. Though she tried to hold him upright, he fell to his knees.

Water. He needed water. Desperately, she dragged him toward the stream.

The fire was so close. Bits of ash swirled in the air. She heard the roar of the flames, the snapping of tree branches.

"What is it?" Liam asked. "What do you remember?"

"Death."

Kate knew what had happened next. The pain and horror would always be with her. Inescapable. "I know why I couldn't remember. It's too terrible."

"You have to tell me," Liam said.

Wayne's cough went silent. The tension left his body. She didn't want to believe he was dead. Against all odds, she fought to save him. If only they could reach the stream...

"Wayne couldn't make it. He stopped breathing. His arms and legs went limp. His face was horrible, sunken. His eyes were dead."

She couldn't continue. Unmindful of the grime, she sank down on the scorched earth. Her arm raised and she pointed toward the remains of a beaver lodge. "Over there. I buried him."

Chapter Nineteen

Amid the burned forest and former beaver ponds, Liam saw a surreal landscape for Kate's visceral memories. He felt her struggle and her horror as though it had been his own experience. He ached for her, for what she'd gone through. This pampered princess had been thrust into hell. She'd dragged a dying man through a forest fire. And she'd failed to save him.

Now, it was up to Liam to complete and verify the picture—to find the man she'd buried.

Following the direction she'd pointed, he went toward the beaver lodge—a pile of charred sticks that resembled the remnants of a bonfire. The stinking miasma of the damp, burned forest shrouded the clear, Colorado sunlight.

The inside of his mouth was dry as cotton. He'd seen death before at funerals and wakes. As an assistant D.A., he'd attended an autopsy. In a clinical sense, he knew there was nothing to fear from the dead. Yet, he'd never before felt such a strong portent warning him to turn back.

Wayne Silverman's body had been here for a month. The corpse would be horrific. But he had to see for himself. He had to know with unshakable certainty that her story was true.

He glanced back over his shoulder toward her. She hadn't moved from the spot where she'd crouched on the ground, frozen in the grip of remembered trauma.

Liam went forward. His boots churned the turbid, muddy water as he splashed through a wide, ankle-deep puddle.

At the edge of the beaver lodge, he saw a dark, ugly shadow. It protruded from beneath a fallen, charred log. It was a man. Scraps of clothing clung to what used to be an arm.

Closer, Liam pushed aside blackened branches. Soot marked his hands. He stared down at the body. The skull was a mummified yellowish brown. The jaw gaped as though caught in a scream.

Though burned and rotted beyond recognition, Liam knew he'd found Wayne Silverman.

There was no need for him to make further identification. That was a job for the forensic experts. A job for the police.

He turned away. The image of that corpse would be with him forever. From the start, he'd suspected that Wayne was dead. Now he knew.

And he had to move on. He returned to Kate and squatted down beside her. "Are you okay?"

"I think so," she said. Her blue eyes were awash in pain. "It's over now."

But it wasn't ended. It wouldn't be over until they knew the identity of the murderer. "Do you remember who shot at you?"

She shook her head.

When he touched her shoulder, he felt her trembling. Her slender, fragile body quaked.

"Now I know," she said, "why I didn't want to remember. It wasn't because I was a thief or because I caused Wayne's death. I couldn't remember because I didn't want to return to what happened here."

Liam understood her reaction, but he was at a loss to reassure her. He couldn't erase the past, couldn't protect her from her own experiences.

Her voice shuddered. "Did you find him?"

"Yes," he said.

"I want him to have a proper grave," she said. "I don't care what he did. If he was a blackmailer or a thief, it doesn't matter. I want to put Wayne Silverman to rest."

Liam helped her to her feet and guided her back the way they had come, leaving the nightmare behind them.

In the Jeep, he tried to call CCC on his cell phone. He wanted to notify Briggs about the exact location of the corpse. It was important for Detective Clauson's case to have access to this body.

But the call wouldn't go through. There was no decent signal from their remote location.

"We could go to Cougar Creek," she suggested. "You could make the call from there."

No way would he go near anyone from RMS or the Carradine family. "We'll go back to my cabin. We can take the chopper from there and return to town."

Their return drive was mostly quiet—the natural aftermath of emotions running high for too long. Liam took this chance to breathe. There was nothing more they could do. He had no other plans for investigation. With the financial data and the body, Clauson surely had enough to build a case. There would be forensics on the corpse; maybe the police would find a traceable bullet. Clauson could track the embezzled funds and come up with a name. Even if Kate never appeared as a witness, there was plenty of circumstantial evidence.

In that sense, she'd been right. It was over. Once the police made an arrest, she'd be safe.

She wouldn't need him to protect her.

Over. It was all over. He'd go back to his regular life at his cabin. She'd go back to her social whirl. And never the twain would meet. More than likely, he would never see her again, never hold her in his arms, never hear her laughter.

But he knew that every time the rain fell, every time he heard the patter of raindrops against his cabin roof, he would think of her. Stormy and wild as a thunderstorm. Refreshing as spring rain. She would always be a part of him.

As they neared his cabin, she asked for the cell phone. "I want to try calling Tom again."

"Why?"

"I can't believe he's involved. Maybe he can give me a decent explanation."

He handed the phone to her. "Don't expect too much."

"When it comes to my extended family," she said, "I've learned to expect the worst."

Kate punched in her stepbrother's phone number and waited while it rang. Much to her surprise, he picked up. "Tom, I'm glad I caught you. You're finally answering your cell."

"Katie? Where did you take off to?"

"I'm fine," she said dismissively. "I need to ask you about something. In the past couple of weeks, did you go to Stanhope Jeweler?"

"Yeah, to get a copy of one of your mom's necklaces. Some diamond thing."

He didn't sound like getting the copy had been any big deal. "Why?"

"An errand," he said. "Just like all the other crappy errands I get sent on. Like I don't have anything else to do with my time."

"Who sent you?"

"What's this about?" The suspicion in his voice was clear, but there was a lot of noise in the background, as if Tom was standing in the middle of a construction site. "Where are you, Katie?"

"It's about Mickey Wheaton," she said. "How is he doing?"

"How would I know?"

"You were friends. You and Mickey and Wayne."

"Listen, Katie, I don't know what you're getting at. But stop it. Haven't you gotten yourself in enough trouble?"

The background noise got even louder. "Where are you, Tom?"

"I needed to get away from the city. I'm at Cougar Creek."

She disconnected the phone call. Tom was here. He was close.

Liam's Jeep bounced along the road to his house. She could see the white wings of his Super Cub. He drove up the hill to his cabin, where the chopper stood waiting. They were minutes away from a clean escape.

"What's wrong?" he asked.

"Tom's at Cougar Creek."

"Good," Liam said. "That means he's not here."

He parked in front of the cabin, climbed out from behind the wheel and stretched. He had been her rock throughout these difficult days. She didn't want to lose him. She should tell him how she really felt.

But a sense of danger rose up inside her, overwhelming all other concerns. Something wasn't right. "We have to get away from here. Now. This minute."

"You bet," Liam said. "I'm going to run inside, grab a couple of candy bars and we're gone."

"Don't go into the house. There's no time."

"Two minutes," he said. "You can wait for me by the chopper."

She wanted to grab hold of him, to stop him from taking one more step. She leaped from the Jeep, watching Liam stride toward his front porch.

Frantically, she scanned the area. What was different? What was out of place?

Her gaze stuck on the hangar behind his plane. She caught a glimpse of another vehicle parked inside. Someone was here. They were hiding, lying in wait.

"Liam!"

When she called to him, he turned toward her.

Her final memory flashed across her mind.

Wayne Silverman came down the steps from the cabin. He walked back to the Explorer, carrying his backpack and smiling. On the porch behind him, she saw a rifle. The shooter took aim. It was Peter Rowe.

The same thing was going to happen to Liam. She could feel it coming.

"Behind you!" she screamed. "On the porch!"

Liam pivoted. He dropped to the ground and dodged as the shooter took aim.

Even from this distance, she recognized the professional assassin who'd attacked at her house in Denver. He held a Winchester rifle. No need for a silencer out here. He fired once, twice.

Liam darted behind a rock. "Get down, Kate."

She ducked behind the Jeep. The cell phone was still in her hand. She called nine-one-one. It rang and rang.

Liam had taken the small handgun from the ankle holster. He angled around to get a shot.

She could only pray that he'd be successful. But he was overmatched. His little .22-caliber automatic was no match for the accuracy and range of the assassin's rifle.

On the cell, the sheriff's dispatcher finally answered, "This is nine-one-one."

"I'm at Liam MacKenzie's cabin," Kate said. "There's a shoot-out. Hurry."

"Please stay on the line, ma'am."

"No time." Kate repeated, "Liam MacKenzie's cabin. Do you know where it is?"

"Yes, ma'am. But I need for you to—"

"Hurry." Kate dropped the phone.

The assassin came down the porch stairs. His pace was cool. His confidence unshakable. Apparently, he didn't know Liam was armed.

Liam stepped out from behind his rock, aimed and fired three bullets.

The other man dropped to his knees. Without a sound, he went facedown in the dirt.

"Kate," Liam called. "Are you okay?"

"Fine."

But she didn't believe they were safe. Her instincts told her that the hunters weren't through with them yet.

As Liam edged cautiously toward the downed man, she held her breath. The assassin wasn't moving. Was this a trick?

If so, Liam was prepared. He held the handgun at the ready. One move from the man on the ground, and she knew he'd fire.

Her heart beat fast as she watched. Careful. Careful. Liam picked up the rifle. The assassin still wasn't moving.

As Liam jogged down the hill toward the Jeep, she saw Peter on the porch. This couldn't be happening. Not again.

Before she could call out, a gunshot exploded. Liam stumbled but he didn't fall. He kept coming toward her, circled the rear of the Jeep. Then, he sank to the ground and leaned his back against the fender. Blood drenched his white shirt from a wound at his shoulder.

She knelt beside him, helpless. Unable to stop the bleeding. Unable to save his life.

"Take the rifle, Kate."

Her hands trembled. She was distraught, caught in the throes of panic. "You're hurt."

Two shots exploded from the porch.

"It's a flesh wound," he said. "A hit in the shoulder. I'll be okay. But I can't aim the rifle. You've got to do it."

"I can't."

With his good hand, he gripped her arm. "Get mad, Kate. Get tough. I know it's in you."

She shook her head. She couldn't go through this again. The terror. The pursuit. The death.

"If you can't shoot," he said, "you've got to run."

Running from the hunters. She'd gone miles. She'd lasted days, weeks. Could she do it again?

"Not this time." Her blood surged. Determination flowed through her body. "I'm not running."

She would never leave Liam here to die at the hands of her stepfather. She planted a quick, hard kiss on his mouth. "I can handle this son of a bitch."

Kate took the rifle, checked the bolt and nested the

barrel against her shoulder. There were only two rounds left. She had to make her shots count.

In the shadows of the porch, she saw Peter Rowe ducked down behind a chair. Not a clear shot.

She wasn't a marksman like her stepbrother, but she knew how to shoot. Taking aim, she squeezed the trigger.

Immediately, Peter fired back.

"Liam, I only have one bullet left."

"I've got four more rounds in the pistol," he said. "See if you can make him come to you."

"How?"

"Negotiate."

She swallowed hard. It was up to her, and she was going to make this work. She called out, "Peter, you win."

"What are you talking about?"

"We give up. You win."

"It's not that simple, Kate. This isn't a golf match."

He sounded nervous, and his fear made her even stronger. "If you let me take Liam to a doctor, we'll disappear. You'll never hear from us again."

"No deals." He darted to the edge of the porch, hopped over the railing. "Silverman tried to make a deal. I paid the filthy little blackmailer. Then, he wanted more."

"I'm not like him." She sighted down the barrel of the rifle, but she couldn't see him. "You can trust me."

"I trust no one."

"Not even Tom?"

"Leave my son out of this," Peter yelled.

In the quiet of the forest, she could hear his every rustling movement. He dodged toward the rock where Liam had taken cover.

She called out to him. "Tom was involved. Tom went to the jeweler to get the copy of the necklace. Mickey Wheaton saw him."

"Mickey was another one who wanted a deal. He was going to start the blackmail all over again. But Tom had nothing to do with this. He was just doing me a favor."

"You bastard!" she shouted. "You sucked your own son into your crimes. Why did you do it, Peter? Didn't you have enough money?"

"I'm sick of living on Carradine family leftovers."

Crouched beside her, Liam held his small pistol in his left hand. Quietly, he said, "You're doing good. Make him angry."

"Why?"

"So he'll make a mistake. We need for him to come out from behind the rock."

She called out again, "You don't deserve a penny of my family's money."

"You spoiled little brat!" Peter yelled. "You don't know what it's like. Me and my son were never good enough for the holier-than-thou Carradines."

"Damn right," she returned.

"I tried to be a good father to you."

Anger flashed through her, but she kept herself in control. "Don't you dare compare yourself to my father. He was good and strong. You're a loser, Peter. Weak. Shallow."

"And you, my dear, are dead."

He stepped out from behind the rock, and she pulled the trigger. Her bullet went wide. She had no more ammunition.

Peter fired once. The bullet clanged against the side of the Jeep. He fired again, marching toward them. Beside her, Liam rose to his feet and took aim. Each shot had to count. Peter was less than ten yards away.

Liam fired. The rifle dropped from Peter's hands.

He staggered. His scream echoed against the cliff sides.

Liam fired again, and Peter fell to the ground, moaning.

"Get his gun," Liam said.

She darted around the Jeep and grabbed the rifle. She didn't spare a single glance for Peter Rowe as he writhed in the dirt. She hoped his pain was intense.

She dashed back to the Jeep, where Liam stood bleeding. He forced a grin.

"Now," he said, "it's over."

From a distance, she heard the approaching wail of the sheriff's siren. They'd made it.

Liam wrapped his good arm around her waist and pulled her close. His face was drawn and pale.

"I'll start first aid on your wound," she said.

"The sheriff is almost here. I'll be fine."

"But I—"

"Not now, Kate. I have something important to say." Wincing, he inhaled a deep breath. "For a minute there, when I got hit, it felt like I was going to die. And I had one thought. Only one."

His eyes were hazy. She could tell that he was at the verge of passing out. "Liam, you don't have to talk."

"All I could think was this—I'm never going to have the chance to love Kate."

She was stunned. Speechless.

"I understand," he said. "Survival takes all kinds of skills. Sometimes it's bare subsistence in the mountains. Sometimes it's dealing with a caterer at a charity event."

His words trailed off, and she could tell that speaking was difficult for him. "You need to sit, Liam. You've lost blood."

With an effort, he focused on her face. "I fell in love with Rain, the natural woman. But I love Kate, too. Even if you are a pain in the butt sometimes. I want you to come and live with me. Here."

"I want that," she said. With all her heart, she wanted to be with him forever. "But I can't give up my work. Will you compromise? Are you willing to come down from your mountaintop occasionally?"

The sheriff's vehicle pulled up beside the Jeep. A deputy leaped from the passenger seat and charged toward them.

Liam didn't have the strength to give her an answer. Instead, he brushed a light kiss on her forehead. Without another word, he allowed himself to be whisked into the rear of the sheriff's vehicle.

TWO NIGHTS LATER, KATE still didn't have her answer from Liam. They'd spoken on the phone once or twice, and she knew his wound was minor.

She'd wanted to go up to his cabin, but she was needed in Denver. Glancing in her bathroom mirror, she patted her hair into place and smoothed the black satin gown she would wear to the summer gala.

Tonight, all her survival skills would be necessary. Her mother would not be attending. She was far too humiliated by Peter's treachery. Elizabeth had visited him once in the hospital where he was recovering. The reason for her visit had been to serve him with divorce papers.

So, it was up to Kate to keep this major charity function operating smoothly. She would put on a smiling face for the attendees, who had paid thousands for tickets. And she would encourage the bidding on the silent auction. All the while, she feared she'd lost the one thing she prized most—her relationship with Liam.

From the downstairs of her house, she heard something. Another reporter? Damn it! When would these people leave her alone?

She grabbed an aluminum baseball bat from her bedroom and started for the stairs.

The sound she heard was music. A song. "Rocky Mountain High." What was going on here?

She dashed down the staircase and across the foyer. There was no one in the front room. Her satin gown rustled as she hurried toward the dining room.

On one of the tines of the antler chandelier that hung above her table was a huge red bow. Suspended from the ribbon was a small, black velvet jewelry box.

She took it down and opened it to find a ring with a single perfect diamond. An engagement ring.

Whirling around, she saw Liam. He wore a simple black tuxedo and a glistening white shirt.

"Will you dance with me?" he asked. "For the next fifty years or so?"

Her heart swelled with joy. "I'd be delighted."

Looking like the most debonair man on the planet, he came toward her. He took the ring and slid it onto her finger. His kiss was pure honey.

"We'll live at your place," she said.

"And we'll come down from the mountaintop occasionally."

When he held her for a waltz and they began to dance, she knew this was where she wanted to be forever—in his arms.

They could be in the city, drinking champagne. Or in the wilderness, foraging for survival foods. It didn't matter. Wherever they were, they would make their own world.

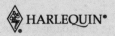

HARLEQUIN®

INTRIGUE®

**Don't miss the third book
in Cassie Miles's exciting miniseries:**

COLORADO CRIME CONSULTANTS

*For this group of concerned citizens,
no mission is impossible!*

ROCKY MOUNTAIN MANEUVERS

BY CASSIE MILES

**Available March 2005
Harlequin Intrigue #832**

When Molly Griffith agreed to go undercover to help out
a friend, her boss Adam Briggs wasn't happy with her plan.
Her investigation turned dangerous, and it was up to the
two of them to find the truth and each other. Would they
realize that some partnerships were meant to last forever?

Available at your favorite retail outlet

HARLEQUIN®
Live the emotion™

www.eHarlequin.com

HIRMM

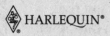

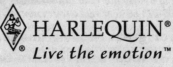

If you enjoyed what you just read,
then we've got an offer you can't resist!

Take 2 bestselling love stories FREE!

Plus get a FREE surprise gift!

Clip this page and mail it to Harlequin Reader Service®

IN U.S.A.	IN CANADA
3010 Walden Ave.	P.O. Box 609
P.O. Box 1867	Fort Erie, Ontario
Buffalo, N.Y. 14240-1867	L2A 5X3

YES! Please send me 2 free Harlequin Intrigue® novels and my free surprise gift. After receiving them, if I don't wish to receive anymore, I can return the shipping statement marked cancel. If I don't cancel, I will receive 4 brand-new novels each month, before they're available in stores! In the U.S.A., bill me at the bargain price of $4.24 plus 25¢ shipping and handling per book and applicable sales tax, if any*. In Canada, bill me at the bargain price of $4.99 plus 25¢ shipping and handling per book and applicable taxes**. That's the complete price and a savings of at least 10% off the cover prices—what a great deal! I understand that accepting the 2 free books and gift places me under no obligation ever to buy any books. I can always return a shipment and cancel at any time. Even if I never buy another book from Harlequin, the 2 free books and gift are mine to keep forever.

181 HDN DZ7N
381 HDN DZ7P

Name	(PLEASE PRINT)	
Address	Apt.#	
City	State/Prov.	Zip/Postal Code

Not valid to current Harlequin Intrigue® subscribers.

Want to try two free books from another series?
Call 1-800-873-8635 or visit www.morefreebooks.com.

* Terms and prices subject to change without notice. Sales tax applicable in N.Y.
** Canadian residents will be charged applicable provincial taxes and GST.
  All orders subject to approval. Offer limited to one per household.
  ® are registered trademarks owned and used by the trademark owner and or its licensee.

INT04R   ©2004 Harlequin Enterprises Limited

like a phantom in the night
comes an exciting promotion from

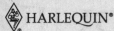

GOTHIC ROMANCE

Look for a provocative
gothic-themed thriller each month
by your favorite Intrigue authors!
Once you surrender to the classic
blend of chilling suspense and
electrifying romance in these
gripping page-turners, there will
be no turning back....

Available wherever Harlequin books are sold.

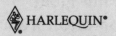